T0113513

A BIRTHDAY OUT OF THIS WORLD

ALLAN KELLY

authorHOUSE®

AuthorHouse™ UK
1663 Liberty Drive
Bloomington, IN 47403 USA
www.authorhouse.co.uk
Phone: UK TFN: 0800 0148641 (Toll Free inside the UK)
*   UK Local: 02036 956322 (+44 20 3695 6322 from outside the UK)*

Published by AuthorHouse 08/06/2021

ISBN: 978-1-6655-8962-8 (sc)
ISBN: 978-1-6655-8961-1 (e)

CHAPTER 1

SCOTT'S BIRTHDAY

Scott's eyes open, and he sees the sun's rays shining through blinds in his bedroom window. He has become a confident young man—even after years of getting bullied at school over his appearance. He is quite short, standing five foot six, and a bit on the chubby side, even after losing a couple of stones of excess weight because he joined the local gym. His shoulder-length ginger hair was one of the reasons behind his constant bullying. He has a few teenage spots still lingering on.

Scott is a happy guy. He always looks on the bright side of life. He has a good job working as a mechanic at the local garage. It's a job he enjoys. Life is good. Scott finds it hard to make friends. He's a bit of a loner. He finds it especially difficult to find a girlfriend.

I'd best get up. This won't get me ready, Scott thinks to himself.

He gets up out of his cosy bed. There's a nip in the air, as there usually is this time of the year in the desert of New Mexico.

Scott makes his way to the bathroom. He gets in the

shower, and warm water flows over his head and body. He starts to imagine what the day ahead will bring.

What will she be like, my first date for ages? I hope she looks like her pictures, Scott thinks. *Karen, that's a nice name.* Karen is only eighteen. She has black shoulder-length hair, a pale complexion, and a slim build and is five foot two. She seems like a nice young lady from a good family. She's a law student. *What would she see in me?* Scott thinks. *Well, this won't do. Daydreaming won't get me ready.*

Getting out of the shower, he dries himself off and uses a quick spray of his deodorant. *How could Karen resist me?* Scott thinks.

As he looks in the mirror, he has a big grin on his face. Making his way into his bedroom, he opens his wardrobe doors. His new jeans and T-shirt hang on the rail. He grabs them, puts them on, and puts his new training shoes on too.

You're looking good Scott, he thinks.

He makes his way into the kitchen and makes himself some cereal and a coffee.

'I can't hang around. I'm meeting her in a couple of hours,' he says to himself.

He makes his way into the hallway, picking up his car keys off a hook on the wall. Glancing at a photo of his parents on the wall, he remembers that it's been two years since they died in a car crash. It was the worst day of Scott's life.

What would they think of me? Would they be proud of me? I think they would, he tells himself.

He grabs his jacket and he heads out the door, locking it behind him. He gets into his car and sets off driving to the petrol station. His thoughts turn again to Karen. Internet dating has a lot to answer for. This will be Scott's first date since his parents died, and he finds himself wondering, *What would they think of her? What will I think of her?*

Well, he told himself, *I will soon find out.*

After a short drive from his apartment, he arrives at the filling station. Pulling up to a stop, he hears a shout.

'Hi Scott! How are you, birthday boy? Are you ready for your big day?'

Scott replies, 'I sure am, Joe. Can you fill the car up? And don't forget; I'm off work next week. Hope you can manage without me.'

'Sure, I'll manage. Hope you have a great birthday and a great holiday. I hope you both get on,' replies Joe.

'Thanks. See you when I get back,' says Scott.

As Scott starts to drive away, Joe shouts and then laughs. 'Hey! Eighty dollars. You can't get away without paying!'

'Oh, sorry, mate. I have too much on my mind. I can't stop thinking about Karen and my holiday,' replied Scott.

'Tell you what, Scott. Have the fuel on me. Happy twenty-first birthday and all the best. Now you best get on your way. You don't want to keep your young lady waiting,' says Joe.

'Thanks, Joe! Catch you later.' Scott waves goodbye.

CHAPTER 2

THE MEETING

Driving out of his small town only takes a few minutes, and then he's on his way on the long desert road heading to Las Vegas. Scott checks his satnav. Only two hours, and he'll be there. *How will I get on with a city girl?* he thinks.

The radio plays, and the miles fly by like the thoughts going through Scott's mind.

Will she have set off already? Will she be on time? Will she turn up at all?

Scott decides to call Karen. 'Hi, Karen! How are you?'

'Hi, Scott! I was just thinking of you. Are you okay?' Karen answers.

'I'm on the highway. Only an hour away from the diner,' says Scott.

'Oh, I'm only half an hour away. I'll wait for you there. Don't rush. I'll have a drink in the diner while I wait for you,' Karen replies jokingly.

'I'm getting a bit nervous about meeting you, Scott,' she adds.

'Don't worry. We'll be fine. I'll see you at the diner. See you soon, love. Take care,' replies Scott.

Driving along the highway, Scott comes across a police roadblock about half a mile ahead. *Oh no, what's wrong?* he wonders. He pulls up at the roadblock.

The police officer says, 'Sorry, sir. The road ahead is closed. There's been a major incident. You will have to take the detour. I'm sorry, sir.'

Scott sets off again. He puts a new route in his satnav, and his eta comes up as forty minutes. *I'd better phone Karen and tell her*, he thinks.

He dials her and tells her he's had to take a detour at the roadblock. He's going to be another forty minutes. Karen laughs. 'Be honest,' she says. 'You don't want to meet me, do you? I'm here now. I'll be drunk by the time you get here.' After a pause, she adds, 'No seriously. Don't worry. Take your time. Be safe. We have all week.'

Scott ignores her advice, and he speeds up, trying to make up for lost time. There's no traffic on the road. In fact, it's eerily quiet. It's a lovely clear sky, and he's making good time, although he's way over the speed limit.

Then out of the blue, there's a big *bang*! The car veers sharply off the road. 'What the hell was that?!' shouts Scott. He's not injured, but he's a bit shaken up. He climbs out of his car. The tyre had blown out, and the car has ended up on its side.

'What a birthday! Could anything else go wrong?' he rants. 'Today of all days!'

He phones Karen and explains what has happened.

She asks Scott, 'Are you all right, love? I will come and get you and help you if I can.' She sets off to pick Scott up.

Back at the crash site, Scott notices it's starting to get darker. The sky is getting dimmer, and the sun is well into setting. It's turning a dull red and starting to touch the horizon. He stands at the side of the road and waits for Karen. Out of the growing darkness, he sees a pair of headlights coming towards him.

'It's Karen!' he shouts, more in hope than certainty.

The car pulls up to a stop by his side.

'Oh, I've never been so glad to see anyone,' he says.

'Me too. I was beginning to think all this was a big wind-up, and you weren't going to show up,' replied Karen. 'Well, I'm here now Don't worry We will be fine.'Replies Scott.

Even in the fading light, Scott could see that Karen was gorgeous and seemed a lovely woman. *This could turn into a good day after all*, he thought.

'What are you going to do about your car, Scott?" asked Karen.

'I'll phone Joe, my boss at work. He'll send a pickup truck from his garage. I'll probably end up fixing it when I get back to work next week,' replies Scott.

Scott phones Joe and explains the situation.

'No problem, Scott. Just glad no one was hurt,' Joe says. 'I'll be there in the next couple of hours.'

'Thanks, Joe. Karen is with me. She came to my rescue,' Scott replies.

'Well, she sounds a good catch. Look after her. It's no use hanging around out there. It's dropping dark now, and it will be getting cold too. I'll see you next week. Don't worry. Enjoy what's left of your birthday and your holiday,' says Joe.

CHAPTER 3

THEIR DATE

'Right, Scott. Jump in,' says Karen. 'We haven't got off to a good start on our first date. But we can get to know each other better now. It won't be long, and you can have your birthday drink and relax.'

'I don't usually except lifts from strangers,' Scott says with a laugh. Well, it is my birthday.' He gets into Karen's car. 'Very nice car,' he says. 'I think you must earn more than a mechanic. Good taste too, a Cadillac. I would never have thought you had a car like this.'

'No,' Karen replies. 'Rich parents.'

'It's been a strange date, Karen. One you won't forget,' says Scott.

They travel down the road, and the miles and minutes fly by. The two of them are talking away and getting on well. It seems like they've known each other for years.

Back down the road at the dinner, when Karen was waiting for Scott, she noticed there were spare rooms. She mentions this to Scott, adding, 'We could stay there if you wanted. I Hope you don't think I'm trying to take advantage of you.' She laughs.

'Well, it is my birthday,' says Scott.

By now, it is pitch-black outside. Scott looks out of the passenger window, and he notices some lights up in the night sky. They're in the distance, flying around erratically. But he doesn't mention it to Karen.

'What birthday sign are you, Scott?' asks Karen.

'I'm a— Stop! Pull over!' shouts Scott.

Karen screeches the car to a stop. In the darkness, only the distant lights in the sky are shinning.

'What's wrong?! What's the matter?' Karen says in surprise.

'I've just seen something at the side of the road. I'm not sure what it was. It looked like someone laid at the side of the road,' replied Scott.

They both get out of the car and run back down the road.

Karen shouts, 'Over here, Scott. There's a man here. He doesn't look too good.'

Scott runs over. He can see a middle-aged man, about 50 years old with a balding head. He's slightly built and only about five feet tall, clean shaven, and wearing blacked-rimmed glasses.

He's barely conscious clothed in black trousers, a white shirt with a blue tie, and a long white gown like a laboratory technician would wear it is badly bloodstained. Altogether, he looks rather worse for wear, a bit beaten up. He's moaning and groaning so quietly his cries are just barely audible.

Karen and Scott crouch down by the man's side. Karen asks, 'Are you all right?'

There is no reply. The man just lays there motionless.

Scott lifts the man's head and cradles him in his arms 'Are you all right?' he repeats.

The man just moans and mumbles. They can't understand him.

Karen runs back to her car and gets a bottle of water. She comes back and gives the man a drink. He seems to respond, and she gives him another sip.

'How are you?' asks Karen

'I'm not too good," he whispers hoarsely. "They're going to kill me if they catch me.'

'Who's going to kill you? Who are you? What's your name?' asks Scott.

No reply from the man.

'Come on, Scott. Help me get him into my car. We have to get him to hospital. We have to get him to safety and cleaned up. He needs medical attention,' says Karen.

They eventually get the man into the car.

'Right, Scott I'm taking him to hospital,' Karen says as she drives off.

'No! No! They'll be looking for me at the hospitals,' says the man with panic in his voice. 'My name is Professor Simon Daniels. Call me Simon. And thank you for stopping and helping me. But you're putting yourselves in danger by helping me. I've been held captive and forced to work at a secret laboratory not far from here.'

'There is nothing around here, Simon,' says Scott.

'Yes, there is. But they're underground, out of sight in a vast complex. It extends over a mile deep underground. There are a few entrances around on the military firing range, all securely fenced off. The entrances are all invisible under the sand and impossible to access. There are many levels, over ten, at the bottom of a mile-deep shaft. We heard that it is fifteen levels deep, but I don't know. It covers a one square mile area.

'I was not abducted. It was more like a trade by the government to work for the aliens down in the complex. The aliens have infiltrated the White House. They're pulling the strings. All our leading scientists and biologists have been traded by the government to the aliens, in exchange for their technology and propulsion systems.

'How do you think we've advanced so rapidly over such a few years—from not being able to fly to landing on the moon in a very short time, from gas lights to nuclear fuel, televisions, microchips, and computers. The list goes on. They've been helping us but at a cost.

'The complex was built over seventy years ago. It was built by humans. But it is owned by the aliens. I specialise in DNA and human biology. I have security clearance to the first ten levels, which start about a mile below the surface. But even I could not go below level ten.

'The government turns a blind eye to the missing person problem all across America. Most end up in there. There are human body parts in what look like big glass tanks filled with blue liquid. There are heads floating in the tanks— heads severed from their bodies but being kept alive. There are hundreds of human clones also being kept alive by intravenous drip feeds into their arms.'

'Oh my God, Simon, you're crazy,' shouts Karen. 'Do you expect us to believe all this rubbish? I think you've escaped from an asylum.'

CHAPTER 4

THEIR ABDUCTION

The argument is abruptly stopped by a deafening sound like thunder from above them. The car is brightly illuminated by a blinding light. Karen brakes hard. The noise grows louder as the lights descend from above them.

'Oh my Lord. They've found me,' cries Simon.

Just then, a large helicopter lands on the road in front of them, blocking the road ahead. A second helicopter lands on the road behind them, blocking their escape route.

The noise of the helicopters' rotor blades is deafening, and the blinding lights make it so they can't see anything.

'Put your hands up,' comes a shout, 'where I can see them!'

'Now slowly get out of the car,' orders another voice, raised above the noise of the rotating blades.

They all obey the orders and are swiftly grabbed, handcuffed, and bundled into the front helicopter. Before they know what's happening, they're flying off through the dark desert sky—low and fast.

In the distance the helicopter that landed behind them, lifts off the ground. It hovers over the empty car. Then a bay door opens, and a metal grabbing device is deployed from the helicopter's belly. The car is lifted up and flown away, leaving no trace of it or its occupants behind.

The helicopters arrive at the top security missile testing range in no time, flying over the perimeter fence. In the front helicopter, the three abductees sit in a huddle, petrified. The helicopters came to a halt, hovering in the air thirty feet above the ground.

Through the open side door, Scott can see the desert sands below, swirling and blowing around due to the downdraught from the rotor blades. Then the ground below started to open up.

What on earth is happening? thinks Scott.

Light becomes visible down in the shaft that just became visible. There are rows of lights of different colours. The helicopter descends into the shaft through different levels, each with different coloured lights for easy identification.

They gently touch down on a landing platform. The rotor blades come to a stop, and all goes quiet.

'Get out!' comes a shout. And with a push in the backs, they are ordered off the helicopter. Scott leads the way. He notices there are no markings on the jet-black helicopter, and it's a kind he hasn't seen before. There is no pilot either. It was like a full-sized drone.

Scott can hear Karen a few steps behind. She is crying. He turns around to comfort her, and as he does, he sees the men who had captured them. There are six of them, three on either side. They're in uniform but not like anything he's seen before. They look military, strangest of all, they look exactly alike—like twins.

'Keep walking, straight ahead,' says one of the guards.

The corridor they're being shepherded down is long, about 100 yards long. It has stainless-steel walls with rows of lights above them on a stainless-steel ceiling. He notices dozens of lifts along the corridor as they walk. They are labelled by level, from 'Level 1' all the way down to 'Level 10'.

CHAPTER 5

INTO THE EARTH

The three captives are led into a large room, about forty feet square. There is darkened glass in the windows, what looks like a map of the complex on the wall, and a large oval table in the middle of the room, with three men sat in big leather swivel chairs. The men are dressed smartly in suits, they sit facing the captive trio.

The man sat in the middle, who looks to be in charge, says, 'Hello, Professor Simon Daniels. How nice to see you again. Did you enjoy your little journey?

'Who are your two friends?'

'I don't know them. I only met them an hour ago. They were going to take me to the hospital,' replies Simon.

'Now, now! Do you expect me to believe that? You would have known we'd have all the hospitals alerted and on the lookout for you. You would never have gone there,' the man in the suit says.

He pauses for a moment. He turns to the other two men, and they have a quiet conversation for a few minutes. Then the leader turns and says to Simon, 'It's a good job we need you—that we need your expertise in your field of genetic engineering and human biology. Or you would be going down to the growing rooms down in the lower levels—with your two friends.'

'No, no! Sir, please don't send them down there. I beg you,' replies Simon.

While this is happening, Scott is looking at the map on the wall, without being too obvious about it. He can see they're in a massive underground complex, with many levels deep underground and hundreds of rooms—just like Simon said when they found him on the desert road earlier. *What if it's true? What if what he was saying about the experiments is true?* thought Scott. Dread fills his mind, and fear grips his body.

Karen stands there like she's in shock, sobbing and shaking. The men at the table are in conversation among themselves again, when suddenly they stand up. The man in the middle gives an abrupt order. 'Take Professor Daniels down to Level 10. Put him back to work on his project. Take the other two down to Level 14.'

The three of them are led out of the room by the guards into the corridor. The guards' expressions never change. They are marched down the long corridor to lift ten. There, one of the guards presses the lift button, the doors open, and they all enter the lift. The lift descends, traveling over a mile down into the earth at high speed.

What is happening? Can this be real? Or is it a nightmare? I hope I wake up soon and realise it's all been a bad dream, Karen thinks to herself.

The lift comes to Level 10. 'Get out!' shouts one of the guards.

They are all pushed out of the lift. 'Keep moving,' comes a shout from a guard.

Karen, Scott, and Simon keep moving down the corridor. It's like the one on the upper level, but it has windows along each side. Inside, there area what looks like aquariums filled with a blue liquid. The rooms are filled with a pale blue mist like a fog. There are lots of high-tech machines inside.

Scott lets out a shout. 'My God!' he cries.

There are people submerged in the tanks of blue liquid. As he walks down the corridor passing windows on either side, he sees other tanks containing human embryos all at different stages of development. Some contain body parts, lungs that are breathing on their own, or beating hearts. Other tanks contain human brains. There are even severed heads still living, with eyes that watch them as they walk by; the looks on their faces will haunt him forever.

Karen screams. She collapses to the floor, shaking and crying. Scott crouches down by her side. Trying to comfort her, he assures her that things will be fine, even though he's not too sure himself.

Simon helps Scott get Karen back on her feet, and they both try to reassure her with words of comfort. They're all escorted down the corridor past even more hideous sights. The guards' expressions never change, as if they're oblivious to everything around them. They have only one goal—to obey their orders.

They come to an office at the end of the corridor. 'We're here. This is my office,' remarks Simon.

They are all bundled into the office.

Karen screams at Simon, 'Why are you doing this? Why are you involved? You are evil, just like them!'

Simon replies, 'I told you. can't you remember. Can't you remember when you found me out in the desert? But you didn't believe me. You said I had escaped from an asylum. This is far worse than any asylum. Now do you believe me?

'I have been brought down here. I have been traded, with the full knowledge of the government. But these alien beings won't keep their side of the bargain. They are only showing us a small part of their technology. They are hundreds of years more advanced than what they are showing us. I know. I have seen some of the things they have. That is why I tried to escape—to warn the world.

'I was hoping to help the world with my work. That was my dream—to benefit humankind. But look what is happening. I am helping to destroy the human race. Alzheimer's, dementia, and mental illness are all becoming more common and widespread. Do you think that's a coincidence? All of this has happened in the last seventy years—ever since they came back to earth. They are planning on manipulating our genes and harvesting us. They need to clean up the atmosphere first though.'

Over the intercom comes a message. 'Take the two captives to Level 12 immediately.'

As Scott and Karen are being led away out of the office, Simon shouts to them, 'Please forgive me. I am sorry.'

Scott and Karen are taken down a corridor past windows where there are babies being put into what looked like incubators with drip feed pipes been inserted into their arms. They pass dozens of rooms filled with the little babies. They come to a lift. A sign above the lift doors says, 'Levels 11 and 12'. The lift door opens. Scott remembers what Simon said when they found him about no one who worked at the complex having been below Level 10. Here they were, seconds away from Level 12. The guards take Karen and Scott into the lift. It descends to Level 12 and comes to a stop. Karen and Scott are ordered out of the lift by the guards. Their handcuffs are removed.

They are out of the lift. The guards keep moving the pair along. It's hot down there and extremely bright—like being on a sunbed. They are taken to a large room. They see a group of small beings—each about four feet tall—approaching them. Karen and Scott can only see their silhouette in the bright light. The beings communicate with the two captives through thought; it's like the beings can read their minds.

They begin to feel light-headed and a bit dizzy. Then a strange feeling comes over them. Suddenly, they began to levitate, floating down the room about three feet in the air in a horizontal position.

They come to rest on what looks like operating theatre examination tables. All around them is eerily quiet. Some robotic arms come out of the tables and remove Scott and Karen's clothes. They're sprayed with a pale orange liquid and washed by what looks like a miniature car wash and then dried off by warm air blowers. The small beings approach the examination tables. They take blood samples, hair samples, and a small piece of skin from each of Karen and Scott's legs. They are injected in the groin. They also have probes inserted up their noses. They felt paralyzed, completely unable to move, but they can hear everything going on around them. They try to scream, but no noise comes out. Above their heads, rows of differently-coloured lights flash like disco lights. The lights suddenly stop and turn red. The next thing they know, they're stood back up at the door they came in through.

Next, the two of them are dressed in some kind of boiler suit outfits of a waterproof material, along with boots that come up to their knees like Wellington boots. The guards move them out of the room they were just examined in and back into another corridor. Passing more windows, they can see what looks like people—only they have six legs. Others have two legs but four arms. Some have two heads, and there are even some who have animal bodies but human heads. Scott and Karen are marched past dozens of windows. In the faint green light, they can see what looks like large fish with human heads in tanks, swimming in a blue liquid

'How have we got into this?' cries Karen.

'It's all my fault. If I hadn't had the accident, none of this would have happened,' replies Scott.

They arrive at another lift. *This place is massive*, thinks Scott.

Above the lift, a sign reads, 'Levels 13 to 15'. One of the guards presses the lift button, and the door opens. 'Get in, you two,' shouts one of the guards.

Karen and Scott get in. They're alone. The lift sets off, moving farther down into what is getting more and more like hell with every passing minute. The lift stops, and Scott notices it's at Level 14. The doors open. A voice that comes from the intercom inside the lift commands, 'Get out of the lift.' They both get out, and the doors close behind them.

CHAPTER 6

MEETING MARY

They stand there alone. Scott holds Karen, giving her a big cuddle. 'We'll be all right,' he tells her. 'Don't worry. We will be fine.'

Karen, who is shaking and crying, doesn't respond.

There is a very strong smell of ammonia and a stench of sewage.

'Oh, I can hardly breathe,' says Karen.

'You will get used to it,' says a voice in the semi-darkness.

'You will get used to the light too,' it says.

'Who are you?' says Scott as he peers in the half-light. He sees the figure of an old woman dressed like him.

'I am Mary. I have been told to show you what to do down here since you failed your test on Level 12.'

'What test?' Karen asks.

Mary answers, 'You will have had a test to see if you were fit for consumption, but you failed. Most do. That's why the lights above your beds turned red.'

'Consumption. What are you talking about?' shouts Karen.

Mary replies, 'The aliens eat human flesh, but we are far

too polluted now, compared to how we used to be years ago when they were last here. There was no pollution back then, no chemicals. We had no food additives in our bodies. They could harvest us at will. They used to come to earth and take away entire communities for food, like the Mayans and the inhabitants of Easter Island. There were many harvests over the centuries.

'That's why you failed the test. You are polluted, contaminated, like every other worker down here—there are many thousands of us. We are all abducted by the aliens. No one looks too hard for us. The government knows what is happening. They don't want to upset our new rulers and have our new technology taken away, which the aliens are giving us. We could not live without it.

'There will come a time not too far from now when the world will get cleaner with clean air because of solar power, wind power, and electric cars. The alien technology is benefitting humankind. But ultimately, it is making us edible for the aliens.

'When that day comes, they will come down and harvest us off the face of the earth and not have to hide underground anymore.

'Oh, what are your names? How rude of me,' says Mary.

'We are Karen and Scott,' replies Karen.

'Right come on then, or you will get us all in trouble,' says Mary.

Mary leads the way down a dimly lit corridor with doors down either side. She opens one of the doors. The room lights up with a glowing red light. The smell inside is terrible. There are rows and rows of naked people. They're all stood up, with about three feet between each of them.

The people are fastened to chrome poles, about two inches in diameter. Tubes are going into their arms, so they can be intravenously fed clean healthy nutrients to make them grow at a rapid rate.

The people in there can't speak. You can only hear shrieks and screaming noises, like the sounds chimps make. Their eyes are wide open and full of fear, but they hardly move—just the odd flailing arm.

'Come on. Follow me,' says Mary.

Mary goes into the room. Scott and Karen follow her in.

'Close the door behind you,' shouts Mary.

Scott does as he is told and closes the door.

Mary presses a button on the wall at the side of the door, and a conveyor is jolted into motion. The people all started travelling on a massive conveyor system. Above them, a sprinkler system washes the people with soap and water as they pass by. The poor people let out moans and groans, growing restless and agitated. Then the conveyor comes to a stop.

'That's them all cleaned up. They're all looking healthy too. Now to feed them,' says Mary.

Mary presses another button on the wall. Liquid is sent into the arms of the people, who are being fed intravenously through the tubes they're attached to.

'Who are these people?' asked Karen.

'They are not people!' Mary shouted. 'I don't have time to explain everything now. I'll tell you later. Now come on. We must hurry,' says Mary. 'We must go now to the sewer below them to make sure the channels are all clear so the excrement and urine flows away.'

The three of them make their way down some metal

stairs and descend into the sewer, clearing the channels with shovels and brushes.

'Okay, everything is good down here. Now let's get back upstairs; there's still a job to do up there,' says Mary.

They make their way back up the stairs and into the room with the human clones. The wash down and feed seems to have made them much more at ease. Only a few quiet murmurs can be heard among them.

'We just have to weigh them now,' Mary says, flicking a switch on the wall. It records the weight of all the clones on the conveyor. A digital read out on the wall lights up— 6,872 kilograms, it registers. Mary remarks, 'That's good— an increase of 80 kilograms since yesterday. Another week, and they'll be ready to be dispatched.'

They make their way through other rooms, noting other abducted workers making their way in and out of other rooms. There are dozens of them. A few hours later, they're on the last room. They've just cleaned out the sewage channels.

Heading back up the stairs, they go into the room of clones. Mary flicks a switch on the wall. The digital read-out says 8,012 kilograms. It flashes and turns green. Then the words 'Ready to dispatch' light up on the screen.

Mary says, 'We will dispatch them tomorrow. There will be twelve rooms to ship off in the morning, nearly one hundred tonnes. Our alien lords will be happy. Well, that's enough for today. Come on, you two. We've finished. You deserve a rest. And to try and come to grips with all that has happened today. I know it's hard. I remember my first day down here.'

'This seems like a nightmare. Please tell me it's not true. Tell me it's not real. I can't live through this,' says Karen.

Scott holds her and says, 'You can do this! Be strong. Mary has managed to get through this. We can too!'

'Yes you will be fine,' Mary says, leading them away. 'I will take you to where you'll be staying.'

'I would rather be dead. This isn't living. It's worse than death,' cries Karen.

'I will get you out of here, Karen. I promise you. If Simon managed to find a way out, so can we,' Scott says.

'No. You can't escape from down here. In the twenty years I've been down here, no one has ever managed to get out,' Mary replied.

They eventually reach their room. Mary opens the door. 'It's not the Ritz, but it's a place to escape from all this madness. Out there those are your beds. There's food and water here too, though it's just enough for us to barely get by on. You just have to try and switch your minds off,' Mary tells them.

As Scott and Karen sit on their beds Mary brings them a bowl of food each and a drink. The food looked a bit like a porridge.

'Uggh! What is it?' asks Karen as she takes a taste.

'Don't ask,' says Mary.

As they sit on their beds, Mary tells them the story of how she was abducted when she was a young woman. She was out in the park one summer, late evening. She was out with three friends. They saw blue sparkling lights up in the sky. They were twinkling for a few minutes. They kept changing in brightness and size—about a dozen of them. Suddenly, they merged together into one large sphere, which then disappeared behind some trees. A few seconds later, it reappeared, directly above the foursome, hovering about sixty feet overhead. 'We were immersed in a bright light that shone on us,' she recalls. 'And then we were lifted up on a beam of light into the craft. The next thing I knew, I was at this complex on an examination table, like you two were earlier. My friends and I spent a few years down here together. Sadly, they all died within six months of each other. We had all been at school together. We had known each other since we were five. Every year in this country, over 100,000 people go missing. Some of them work on the ferry crafts. Some are taken somewhere else. I don't know where.'

'I'm not with you, Mary. Ferry crafts? What do you mean?' asks Karen.

'You'll see tomorrow. But you must get some sleep. You both have a busy day ahead of you tomorrow,' replies Mary.

They all eventually fall asleep from exhaustion. But as tired as they are, Karen and Scott keep waking up and shouting out in a cold sweat. They wake a few times thinking it's all been a bad dream—only to realise it's all too real, that just a few feet away there are hundreds of cloned beings in rooms. They eventually fall back to sleep due to sheer exhaustion.

CHAPTER 7

A DAY IN HELL

Morning comes, and it's another day in hell for Karen and Scott. There is no sunrise for them—nothing to tell them it's the start of another day. Only the flashing lights above their beds are there to wake them.

Mary shakes Karen and Scott, 'Wake up! Wake up! We need to eat and get to work,' she says.

They quickly have their bowl of vile food and a mug of water.

Mary says, 'Come on. We best get going. Come on. Follow me.'

They go out into Level 14's corridor. They see other abductees like themselves, hurrying around, like worker ants going in and out of the dozens of rooms all along the long corridor containing all those soulless human clones to wash them, feed them, and clean out all their waste—like they do every day.

'We are on the same rooms as yesterday,' Mary tells her two new helpers. 'You'll be fine. Just do like I tell you. You will come to know what to do.'

Mary opens the door to the first room. The smell is

overpowering. And the noises coming from within—the screams and screeches of the poor tormented clones—are horrendous. The rows of eyes stare as they enter the room.

Mary starts the conveyor to wash the clones down. As she does she shouts, 'Oh no! It looks like one in the third row has an infection. Something is wrong with her right shoulder. It might be some kind of disease. She must be disposed of.'

Mary finishes the washing process, the clones' wide-open eyes staring at her. Some thrash about like fish out of water, even though their bodies are fastened to restraining poles.

'Watch,' shouts Mary to her two helpers.

She climbs through the guard rails in to the rows of clones. They become more agitated, some screaming out. Mary makes her way through the rows, trying to avoid the intravenous tubes. When she gets to the infected clone, she examines it closely. She sees that, under the clone's skin, there is movement, and from a small cut, maggots are crawling out.

'Now watch,' shouts Mary over the din. 'Can you see?' she asks, making sure Scott and Karen are paying attention.

'Yes,' they reply.

They peer through the rows of clones, Mary shows them how to disconnect the intravenous feeding pipes and block the ends so as not to waste the precious feeding fluid. 'Did you see what I did?' asks Mary.

'Yes, we did,' comes the reply.

'Now watch carefully,' says Mary. She pulls a lever at the side of the diseased maggot-infested clone. A trap door opens below the clone, and it plunges down into the sewage and filth below with a big splash.

Karen notices eyes looking up from below and sees movement. 'There are people down there,' she cries.

The people in the sewer system are barely alive. They move stooped over and are just skin and bone. They are wallowing in the stench and filth.

'It's their job to dispose of the rotten crop and keep the sewage channels open,' replies Mary.

Mary makes her way back through the clones and back over the barrier. She gives herself a quick wipe down. 'I don't want to catch anything,' she says.

Mary turns on the feeding machines to feed the clones and then turns on the scales to see what the weight of the crop is today.

'Oh, even though we've lost one there, is a slight weight increase. She was a skinny one anyway,' says Mary.

'I can't believe you said that, Mary' screams Karen. 'You are becoming inhuman, heartless, soulless, just like the clones.'

'How do you think I've survived so long down here?' Mary retorts, her voice raised. 'You can't have feelings. You just have to think about yourself.'

'Now come on. Pull yourselves together, or you will end up down there with the rotten clones and sewage. Believe me. I've seen it countless times. These guards have no feelings. They are genetically programmed to follow orders. They are the pick of the crop, saved from transportation and consumption by the aliens. They don't know it, but they are the relatively luck ones.'

Mary looks pointedly at Karen and Scott. 'Hurry now.

We have to get the alien craft loaded up. They're just about to dock. You see how that light above the loading bay door has just turned amber. We have to get moving.'

The loading bay doors lift up, and they can see a large circular area with dozens of open loading bay doors all around its edge. When they look up, they see a large silver metallic object, like a giant doughnut, hovering about forty feet in the air. The craft is absolutely silent as it slowly descends towards them. The hairs on the backs of their necks stand up. Still making no sound, the craft comes to rest level with the loading bay door.

A door on the craft slowly and noiselessly opens. Looking inside, Scott and Karen see a dim hazy yellow light and alien beings, light grey in colour with slender bodies, large heads, and big black eyes.

Scott stands there in disbelief. *I have heard so many stores about the grey aliens. They really do exist. It's unbelievable everything that's happening*, he thinks.

Out of the alien craft comes a metal conveyor, similar to the one in the growing room that the clones stood on. It's telescopic and is now extending towards the room with the clones.

Mary opens a door to allow the two conveyors to connect; there is a click as they join together. Mary turns off the machine that is feeding the clones, while Scott and Karen disconnect the tubes fastened to the clones' arms. The conveyor starts moving, transferring the clones out of the growing room and into the alien craft. The clones scream and let out long howling screeches, their eyes wide open and bulging.

As the last few clones are loaded on board the craft,

Scott sees it's filling up with hundreds of clones being loaded through dozens of doors all around the craft.

'Where do these people come from?' asks Karen. 'You said you would tell me, Mary.'

'They are not people. They are cloned!' Mary shouts angrily. 'They are cloned beings, grown in growing tanks from embryos, tanks filled with blue fluid on the upper levels. They emerge from the tanks of sticky fluid as new-born babies. They get placed in the first room, fastened to poles, and attached to feeding tubes.

'When I first came to the complex, that was where I worked—on the upper levels. It was heart breaking seeing the little babies. They gradually get moved along the system, going from toddlers to teenagers, all fastened to poles and fed in the growing rooms.

'Mercifully, they know no better. They're like battery hens, not knowing the outside world—until, as you've seen, they end up here being transported.'

With that, another day in the growing rooms below the earth is over. 'Let's get back to our rooms.' The tired remark comes from Mary. They make their way back to their room and get cleaned up in silence.

'This is a good place I have here compared to most,' Mary tells them. 'And I have it because I have proved to be a good worker and a loyal servant. I have grown accustomed to my place, just like all of humanity will have to get used to whatever the aliens have in store for us.'

'They will never win!' shouts Scott.

'They already have,' says Mary in a quiet dejected voice.

'The clones that were loaded onto the alien craft. Where do they go?' asks Scott.

'No one knows, could be anywhere. They will be food for the crew. But there is too much for one ship to eat. And the number of clones being transported is increasing each year, so I think the alien population out there is growing,' replies Mary.

'The greys eat human flesh?' asks Scott.

'They only eat the cloned humans. We would kill them with all the toxins in our bodies due to the pollution in the atmosphere and the bad food we eat with drugs and chemicals in it. That's why we have to look after the clones and rear them disease free.

'The greys are just scouts for a more powerful warlike race that has been traveling the galaxy for thousands of years. We must be a good food source. They have kept coming back. But we have upset them by polluting the world and the planet's atmosphere so much and, by doing so, polluting their food—us!' Mary tells Scott.

'I have a plan, a way of getting out of here. I don't know what the outcome will be. But at least we will not die in this godforsaken pit. Will you help us, Mary?' asks Scott.

'I'm not sure. What's your plan?' replies Mary.

They talk long into the night. Eventually Mary agrees to help Karen and Scott escape but says she will stay, it would make it easier for them and that she doesn't think she has much longer to live anyway.

Karen and Scott both fall asleep dreaming of their escape and freedom.

CHAPTER 8

BID FOR FREEDOM

They are awakened once more by the light above their beds. It's the same old disgusting slop for breakfast. Scott and Karen force it down.

'Well, today is the day. Are you sure you want to go through with it, Karen?' Scott says.

'I'm sure,' replies Karen.

'Mary, are you sure you want to help and be left behind?'

'Yes I'm sure,' Mary replies.

'Come on then. Let's do it!' shouts Scott.

They all go out of their room and into the corridor—hopefully, at least for Karen and Scott, for the last time. One way or another, this will be Scott and Karen's last day down here on Level 14. 'We will get out or die trying,' both vow to Mary.

They work their way through the day as normal, making it to the last room just as the amber light comes on above the loading bay door.

'They are here to collect their cargo. They are ready to dispatch,' shouts Mary.

The alien craft starts to descend towards them down the

shaft to the loading bay. Mary opens the loading bay door. 'Quick! It's descending!' she shouts.

Scott and Karen make their way into the rows of clones. They start to disconnect the feeding tubes attached to the clones' arms.

Meanwhile, Mary has started the washing process. 'Hurry! Get your clothes off quickly,' she shouts.

Scott and Karen strip off their clothes. They see a male and female clone stood side by side; they looked so pitiful. Karen stands there looking at them with tears streaming down her face.

'Hurry up! Pull the levers,' shouts Mary.

Scott pulls the levers at the side of the two clones. They plummet through the trap doors into the sewage and filth below with two big splashes. Karen and Scott throw their clothes down after the clones and close the trap door again. They take the places of the two clones on the conveyor, standing there motionless and staring straight ahead as Mary starts the conveyor, and the loading process begins, slowly filling the alien craft.

Mary whispers, 'God bless you both,' as the two pass by and enter the craft. The conveyor stops, and everything goes quiet. The pair are on board the alien craft, among hundreds of clones, all packed in like cattle in a cattle truck going to market. The doors all around the craft silently close.

They look around at the hundreds of moaning, screaming, and writhing clones.

Scott thinks to himself, *Out of one hellhole and into another. Out of the frying pan and into the fire comes to mind. Have I done the right thing?* He whispers to Karen, 'We got out. I promised you I would get you out of there. That's the hard part done. We will be fine.'

In truth, he wasn't too sure; he was just trying to reassure Karen.

Suddenly, they hear a low-pitched humming sound, only just audible. The alien craft slowly lifts off the ground. As if by magic, windows start to appear as though parts of the craft have just become see-through. As the craft slowly lifts higher, Scott and Karen see the rows of coloured lights they saw on the way in down the shaft.

How they wish they could go back in time before that day, Scott's twenty-first birthday. The alien craft came out of the shaft. It's dark, like the night they were first taken down into the complex. Then the craft shoots up vertically at tremendous speed into the night sky. They can see lights on the ground. The lights become more widespread, and they can see towns and cities and then whole states. Before long, North America became visible, and the next minute, they are looking at all of the Americas and then the whole world. It is glowing like a glittering orb in space.

The world gets smaller and smaller as they travel through space at tremendous speed. They can see that they are approaching the moon; it grows bigger with each passing second. What kind of craft is this that can travel from the earth to the moon in just a few minutes? Before they know it, the earth is disappearing from view as the alien craft moves behind the moon.

CHAPTER 9

LIFE IN A NEW WORLD

They began to descend to the surface of the dark side of the moon—away from the prying eyes on earth. A massive crater comes into view below them. It begins to open up, like the roof on a football stadium. The craft descends into the interior of the moon—into a vast city maybe the size of New York with dome structures and high-rise buildings of a glass-like material. Scott and Karen see many spacecraft flying around too and fro above the city beneath the moon's surface.

The moon looks like such an empty and desolate place when viewed from earth. Who would ever have known the strange things going on below its desolate surface?

The craft reaches a tall building that stretches at least 1000 feet into the sky of the moon city. There are symbols down the side of the building, all illuminated, that look like hieroglyphs. The craft hovers for a few minutes and then gently descends and lands on top of the tower, quietly and smoothly.

The doors around the alien craft all open. Karen and Scott feel a small jerk as the conveyor they are standing on suddenly comes to life below their feet. The rows of clones in front of them starts moving out of the doors. Karen and Scott are near the end of the line. Their minds are working overtime, imagining all kinds of things.

After what seems a lifetime, the pair emerge from the craft, slowly moving forwards into the alien building and the unknown. They can't believe their eyes. About fifty yards in front of them, the clones are passing by a machine with lasers on it—very high-powered lasers that are cutting the heads off the clones as they are sent passed it on the conveyor belt. From down the line in front of them, they can hear a constant repetitive thud. *Thud, thud, thud*, sound from the heads of the clones as they are lobbed off, dropping onto shoots, and then slide into collecting bins.

The bins are gradually filling up with human heads, with hundreds of eyes staring out at them both. The beheaded bodies are then grabbed by the ankles and suspended upside down. From there, the bodies travel on an overhead track like a monorail, still twitching and blood pouring out of them and being collected in massive containers holding gallons of blood.

Karen and Scott look on, petrified in disbelief. They remain as calm as they can so as not to draw attention to themselves. Scott looks up and sees that there are grey aliens looking down on them from what looks like control rooms up above them. They are overseeing the gruesome proceedings. The pair pass rows of machinery with flashing lights like hieroglyphs and what looks like advanced computers.

Scott whispers to Karen, 'Look. There are workers here like us. They're wearing work clothes like the ones we had on down in the growing rooms in the complex. Looking farther along the conveyor line, they see rooms of beheaded corpses hung up on meat hooks and workers frantically chopping limbs off the corpses as though their lives depend on it. Dozens of arms and legs are piling up all around the blood-spattered workers. As they near the laser decapitators, another room comes into view. Scott notices sets of overalls hung up inside on pegs and pairs of boots. The pair carry on, moving along the conveyor closer and closer to the laser machine and a gruesome death.

When the conveyor moves towards a short tunnel just before the lasers, Scott whispers, 'Come on, Karen. This is our chance. We have to take it. It looks like we'll be in the tunnel for less than a minute.'

Inside the tunnel, Scott sees it's even shorter than he hoped—only about twenty-five feet long. But it's dark inside. Scott whispers, 'Come on, Karen. Jump off the conveyor.'

The two of them jump off the conveyor inside the dark tunnel, which looks like some kind of metal detector. They hope they are out of sight of the aliens' eyes.

'Aaargh! Who are you? What's happening? Clones that walk! That's not possible,' shouts the worker inside the tunnel, the panic in her voice clear and fear in her eyes visible.

Karen and Scott stand there naked, shocked and surprised by their unexpected meeting.

'Please, please don't be upset,' Scott says. 'Don't panic. We won't hurt you.'

'We are people just like you,' Karen adds.

They start to explain what they've been through and how they've come to be here on the dark side of the moon.

The worker stands there listening as the clones continue on their way to the lasers and a gruesome death.

'What's your name?' asks Karen.

'My name is Anne. I'm thirty years old. And I'm from England,' the still shocked worker replies. 'I didn't know where I was taken.' Anne then tells what is now becoming a familiar story of being abducted. 'I didn't realise I was on the moon. That's the last place I thought I would be. I just remember waking up in this in this complex with these clothes on and with all these people from all over the world all telling the same story of being abducted and of having tests done on them.'

Scott asks, 'Anne I saw back down there in a room some overalls hanging on pegs. Do you think you would be able to get us some?'

'I will get you some. Don't worry,' replies Anne.

Anne gets a container box on wheels and pushes it over to the room with the overalls. She puts two sets in the container, along with two pairs of boots. Then she wheels them back to the tunnel where Scott and Karen are waiting anxiously.

'Oh brilliant,' says Karen. 'A good fit too,' she adds as she and Scott get dressed into their work clothes. 'We will blend in well.'

Having changed into the work clothes, they both feel a good sense of relief—having not only escaped from the conveyor belt without being detected but also survived a near-death encounter.

'Follow me,' Anne instructed. 'Stay close and mingle in with the other workers. They are all good people like us, just terrified and wanting to go back home.'

The three watch as the last of the clones come off the alien craft and travel down the conveyor belt to the lasers.

They are all killed and butchered in the food factory, the only food source and means of survival for the aliens.

Anne says, 'Keep quiet. Don't say anything. Keep by my side and keep a low profile.'

The trio sets off, heading down towards the restroom and living area. As they go, they mingle in with other workers as best they can.

Making their way down to the bottom of the production line, they can feel the alien eyes watching them from the rooms up above them. Karen feels sure they've been noticed, but it is just paranoia. Scott whispers, 'Keep strong, Karen.'

They all arrive at the restroom. Anne introduces Scott and Karen to a few of her trusted friends. Scott tells them how he and Karen ended up here, of the growing rooms back down on earth and of the old woman called Mary who helped them to escape. He explains that they took a big gamble, even though they didn't know where they were escaping to and that they didn't care. They thought that anywhere was better than being down there in the growing rooms. But now they aren't too sure.

Karen wonders how Mary is, what has become of her, and if their escape has been discovered. She hopes Mary is safe and well—or as well as anyone can be down in the growing rooms.

It is better that she doesn't know the truth, because Mary has been disposed of down one of the trap doors, having become too ill to work.

Karen tells Anne and her friends about Professor Simon Daniels and wonders how he is down on earth in his laboratory.

CHAPTER 10

PREPARING TO INVADE

Simon is working on a plan, a secret project to try and wipe out the aliens. He has developed a virus that lies dormant and is not detectable for two weeks. Then it will strike with death, stopping all the vital organs within hours.

He has been putting the virus into the feeding fluid the clones are given intravenously. He makes sure they're fed the virus-containing bags in the last room before they're dispatched. That way, the virus won't affect the clones before they're butchered but will remain in their bodies and contaminate them, and the disease will be passed on to the aliens once the clones have been consumed.

It is humankind's only hope, and Simon hopes it works. He feels that an alien invasion is imminent and that it's only a matter of time before he and his plan get found out by the aliens.

***

Back on the moon complex, there is a gathering of the aliens. They've assembled an enormous fleet of spaceships that look warlike and are making plans to invade the earth. It looks like the invasion will be soon, because of all the activity.

Alien supply crafts are being loaded with cloned body parts to keep the invasion force fed. And a different type of alien—enormous, warlike, and very aggressive—is also getting ready to invade earth. Their crafts are full of high-tech weapon systems. They're loading everything they need for the attack—and to conquer the world.

Conditions are perfect now on earth for the invasion. Everything has come to a standstill. The aliens contaminated the planet with a virus a month earlier, bringing human activity to a stop and enabling them to clean up the world and the atmosphere. Pollution has stopped, and soon the aliens will be able to launch their attack on humankind.

Back in the complex, Karen and Scott are eating and talking with Anne and her trusted friends when a group of grey aliens enter the room. There are some guards with them, and the aliens are looking all around ominously.

'My God, they've found us,' Karen whispers.

'Keep calm, Karen,' says Scott soothingly.

'Do you think they know about us?' she asks.

'I'm not sure,' he replies. 'Please just relax. Act normal.'

The aliens point at the group sat around the table. Karen's heart is beating fast and loud. The guards come over to them and lead them out of the restroom. They are marched off to one of the alien crafts. Once they've been put on board the craft, it begins to lift up slowly. As it does, windows appear in the walls of the spacecraft. Through the windows, Karen and Scott can see the complex getting smaller below them as they speed vertically back through the open crater and up into space, leaving the moon behind.

They see thousands of other crafts for as far as the eye can see, all heading to earth. As they come out from behind the dark side of the moon, the earth suddenly comes into view.

Scott looks around and notices that, instead of the normal cargo of clones, this craft is full of a different type of alien—creatures that are much more warlike and aggressive than the grey aliens. These new beings stand over eight feet tall and are covered in scales all over their bodies. They have huge powerful legs that resemble kangaroo legs and are very powerful looking. The upper half of their torsos are similar to large silver back gorillas with large humanlike hands. Their giant heads make Karen and Scott think of a praying mantis. And they're covered in scales like armadillos. Overall, they look very menacing and very eager to get on with the battle and start a new life on a new world. *Ours!* Scott gulps.

The giant aliens are communicating with a strange chattering sound, similar to the noises crickets make. It sounds aggressive and loud. Some of them are standing around in groups eating body parts of the clones, chewing on human arms and legs. They could devour a leg in a few minutes and would throw the bones into piles for the workers to clear away. They have weapons over their shoulders—some kind of laser.

Scott looks out of the window. He can see the earth growing larger every second. It's a sight he thought he would never see again—a sight he longed for. But he hoped it would be under happier circumstances. He feels sorry for the unsuspecting inhabitants of the earth. What will their fate be?

CHAPTER 11

THE BATTLE BEGINS

Within a few minutes, the enormous fleet of alien crafts has entered the earth's atmosphere. It happens so fast there is no time for the world's military leaders to launch missiles to defend the earth. The crafts land within seconds of entering the atmosphere, it was like they just appeared out of thin air. The doors all around the crafts open. The hordes of horrendous beings go bounding out, traveling at tremendous speed, with their big powerful legs eating up the ground.

The giant alien beings are bounding along in thirty-foot strides, able to cover a mile in less than a minute. And they can jump ten feet high with ease. There are hundreds of thousands of them in every continent of the world, running rampant, with nothing to stop them. Before anyone realises what is happening, they have slaughtered thousands of people. The slaughter is merciless—men, women, and children cut down by the aliens with their laser weapons. The smell of burning flesh is awful. Women and children are running away and screaming. Groups of men band together to fight the aliens, but it's of no use; they are no match for the giant aliens.

Scott and Karen can see all the carnage through one of the doors, where they remain frozen in fear, their eyes streaming with tears, wondering if this is the end of humanity.

During the first day of the invasion, the human death toll is in the millions. It's just a matter of time before the aliens conquer the world. It will be a clean new world—a world where they can grow their human crop. They will be free range without pollution, infection, or disease. The aliens won't need to grow clones underground anymore; they'll harvest people grown naturally. Then they'll send for more of their kind from across the galaxy; it will be a new world and a new home for them.

Slaughter goes on day and night. The military finally launches a counter-attack but to no avail. The best fighter jets that the nations of the world have are shot down with ease. Aircraft carriers, ships, and submarines are blasted and sunk by the alien ships with their far superior technology and powerful laser power.

People are panicking as they see their militaries being wiped out. Cities all around the world are emptying, as people flee to the mountains, plains, and deserts, seeking out anywhere isolated to try and escape the slaughter. But wherever they go, they're hunted down ruthlessly.

Then on the fifth day of the invasion, the aliens begin to collapse in agony, frothing at the mouth. They break out in rashes with weeping blisters all over their bodies. Then suddenly the alien crafts start flying erratically and falling out of the skies. It's as if it's raining alien crafts all around. They come crashing down to earth, exploding in flames.

People come out of their hiding places, dirty and bedraggled but with big smiles on their faces, shouting and cheering.

Down in the complex below the desert, Simon is oblivious to what's happening all around the world up above. He realises that his virus is working, though, as, all around the complex, he sees the aliens collapsing and dying agonising deaths. *They are getting what they deserve*, he thinks.

He hopes the virus is working on the clones that were dispatched—*wherever they might be*, he thought.

He has received no orders from the grey aliens for twelve hours now. So he presumes they're all dead. He can see the guards, having no orders to follow, wandering around like lost sheep. He decides to take a chance and goes down in the lift to the lower levels to check how things are. He gets a key off a dead grey alien to operate the lifts.

He goes down in the lift, making

his way along the corridors, and comes across the workers. He explains what he's done with the clones, how he's poisoned the aliens, and that everyone is free to escape. A large cheer erupts, echoing all around the corridors on every level. Before long, word has travelled all around the complex.

Simon leads the way out, showing the workers the way. On the way through the complex, the workers run riot. They smash all the tanks and let the liquid and vile content escape. They destroy all the machines and computers. Simon thinks about all the clones in the growing rooms and decides to kill them humanely. He puts a drug into their fluid and administers it to them, and they all die a peaceful death—much better than the fate that would have awaited them on the moon.

Simon and the workers all eventually make their way out of the complex and out into freedom and fresh air. They see a crashed alien craft in the desert with a few of the giant aliens dead around it.

***

It's all over on the moon. The last alien died yesterday. The workers are all alive in the complex, dead aliens all around. The killing machines of the production line all quiet, they turn their thoughts to the earth, their only hope of rescue, and hope that the aliens down there have met the same fate as their captors.

***

On earth, the last alien has just died, and the last alien craft has fallen from the sky. Its pilot and crew has died from the virus Simon created.

Scott, Karen, Anne, and her friends emerge from the craft. They breathe in the fresh air and feel their feet back on earth. Their thoughts turn to the words Simon said when they were below the desert in the complex. 'I was hoping to help the world with my work.' Well he certainly did. He saved it.

As night begins to fall, a big full moon starts to rise in the night sky. Karen looks up, holding Scott's hand. 'We can't leave them there, can we?' she says.

CHAPTER 12

A BRAVE NEW WORLD

Karen, Scott, and Anne stand there watching the big full moon rise over a new world that has changed forever. 'Louise! Alice!' Anne shouted her two friends. 'Come and see the moon.'

The two young women come over. Louise, who's 25, has long shoulder-length dark hair, stands five foot two, has a fair complexion, and is very pretty. She's a bit on the quiet side; in fact, she rarely speaks. Louise was a factory worker in a bakery in Paris before her abduction five years ago.

Alice is tall, about five foot ten, and thin and has short blond hair. She was only 17 and still at college when she was taken, and she wants to be a nurse. Unlike Louise, she's a chatterbox and has an opinion on everything.

The five of them talk about all they've been through and all that has happened to them. They can hardly believe it.

'We are all so lucky to be alive,' says Scott.

'Yes,' agrees Karen. 'We should pray and thank God for saving us and praise Him.'

They form a huddle, and Karen leads them in prayer.

Afterwards, they all look back at the moon, their thoughts turning back to the complex and all the workers up there.

Scott says, 'I wonder how they are up there. I don't know how long they can survive. But we can't leave them there to die. We must try and help them somehow.'

'Yes, we must do something,' says Alice. 'We can't leave them to die up there.'

Karen agrees. 'The only way is to go back to the moon in one of the alien crafts. But I don't know how we'll be able to manage that.'

They all walked back to the craft that has just brought them back to earth. It's a warm evening, with a gentle breeze blowing and the sweet smell of flowers in bloom.

They get to the ramp and cautiously walk up into the craft. There, they all have a good look around, having only been in the cargo hold before. Scott leads the way around the craft, finally heading up into the flight control room. He has a basic idea of mechanics, but he had absolutely no idea about this craft. All the instrument panels and screens are blank, and symbols that look like hieroglyphs virtually cover the instrument panels. If he could understand them, he might stand a chance.

But he just stood there, looking bemused, like a caveman would look in the front seat of a car. After a few hours, they realise they'll never be able to start the craft, never mind getting it to fly to the moon and back.

As they go back down into the craft's cargo area, down the ramp, and back into the desert, Anne, Alice, and Louise discuss the situation. They're speaking in French, so Scott and Karen don't quite follow, but it soon becomes clear that the friends are arguing and that the conversation is getting heated.

Scott and Karen follow the group out into the desert—a beautiful landscape dotted with tall cactus, sprawling trees, and tufts of desert grass.

Karen says to Scott, 'I've never seen anywhere as nice as this. Where do you think we are?'

'I'm not sure, love,' Scott replies. 'We could be anywhere in the world.'

The three women stop their arguing. They share a group hug and look happy. Anne walks over to Karen and Scott with tears in her eyes. She puts her arms around them both and says, 'I'm sorry, but we've all decided we're going to make our way home. I'm going back to England, and Louise and Alice are going back to France.'

'Yes, I understand what you're saying, Anne,' Scott says. 'But you don't know where we are. It seems we would be better off staying together until we find out where we are. Then we can go our own way. At the moment, we need to stay together; there's safety in numbers.'

'I want to go back home, too—to Las Vegas,' Karen says. 'I want to try and find my parents. I want to know what has happened to them.' Tears flood down her face.

Scott holds her tightly. He looks into her tear-filled eyes and says, 'Karen, I promise you I will do all I can to help you find your parents and get us all back to safety.'

'Right,' Anne says. 'We'd best try and get some sleep for a few hours before morning.'

They make their way back on board the craft and get settled as best they can. Then dropping off to sleep one by one, they settle in for a few hours of sleep before morning.

When they awake, they're all pleased to find they've had the best night's sleep ever. Knowing they're back on earth, free from the tyranny of their alien rulers, and away from the terrible slaughterhouse on the moon has done wonders for their ability to rest.

During the night, Louise noticed that the stars are different from the ones she normally looked up at when she was doing her amateur astronomy. She's seen these constellations before in her books but never in real life.

Louise tells the group what she's noticed—that they're in the southern hemisphere. They all agree that Louise is right.

'We'd best just keep heading north until we find some landmark or evidence of where we are,' Scott says.

CHAPTER 13

HEADING FOR HOME

Just before dawn, they all wake up. After gathering some food and water from the craft's storeroom, they set off on their journey to who knows where. All they know is to keep heading north, and they wonder what they might find along the way.

They see plenty of plants and fauna, and the colour of the sand is beautiful, changing from ochre to grey as they travel along. Vultures and eagles screech in the air; the only things in the sky now, these birds of prey ruled the desert skies. They come across beautiful butterflies, moths, spiders, and lizards; they even see the odd wild goat.

Trees, bushes, and cacti cover the eroded desert floor—a beautiful landscape. And quite a few insects are flying and crawling around. It would be a nice place to be if they hadn't been in such a predicament.

When they've been walking for about three hours, Anne says, 'Can we take a break from the endless walking? I'm getting a bit tired.'

They all agree and sit in the shade under a large tree.

'I'm too hot,' Karen says. 'I need to do something about these overalls.'

Scott finds a sharp stone like a flint and uses it to cut the legs off the overalls, making them into shorts; he cuts the arms off too.

They all feel much better as Scott passes around some bottles of water. They sit for a while drinking, resting, and chatting about their journey.

Suddenly, Anne says, 'What's that over there?'

In a clearing about 400 yards away, she can see something shining. It's a reflection of the sun off something metallic. They all get back to their feet and slowly walk towards the bright twinkling light, just visible through the leaves of a tree standing in the foreground.

As they get closer, Scott shouts, 'It's a small plane.'

It's a Cessna 172—a four-seater light aircraft. As they slowly approach the small plane, Anne says, 'Look, there's a man in the cockpit.'

It's the pilot, and he's slumped over the controls. He has a gash on his head and is badly bruised, and he has a bloody nose.

Scott opens the plane's door; it's quite small inside the cockpit. The pilot sits there motionless. He's a young man, about thirty years old. He has dark shoulder-length hair; is well built, quite muscular, in fact; and sports a neatly trimmed beard. He's wearing a red T-shirt with denim jeans and white trainers.

The man is breathing but motionless. Scott can't see any other injuries on the man. By now, the sun has gotten pretty high in the morning sky, and it's getting hotter by the hour.

Scott gives the man a shake, and the man jumps up

with surprise and shock. He asks what happened. Karen gives the pilot a drink of water and starts to explain about the alien invasion.

'Oh yes! Now I remember!' says the man.

'What's your name?' asks Karen.

'My name is Samuel,' he says, clearly quite agitated. 'I was flying my plane from Bogotá to Neiva. I was carrying a cargo of cocaine. I'm not proud of what I do, but I got involved with a bad gang, and my family's lives are at risk if I don't work for them. So I have to do drug runs for them. I drop the drugs off by parachute out in the desert, and other gang members pick the packages up at night.'

'Where are we?' asks Scott.

'We're in the Tatacoa Desert in Colombia,' Samuel says. 'Where are you going?'

'Karen and I are trying to get to Las Vegas,' Scott says. 'But the three girls are trying to get to France and England.' Scott went on to explain that Karen's family lives in Las Vegas. He tells Samuel about the complex under the desert in New Mexico and the base on the moon. He says they have been moving north, not knowing where they are.

'I could take you to Las Vegas,' Samuel offers. 'But I'll need to refuel at Neiva Airport. It's not far from here. I was lucky to land without damaging anything. I saw some military jet fighters. There was six of them, and they were involved in an air battle with a large object shaped like a flying saucer. It was flying at an amazing speed in all directions. The alien craft shot down the fighter jets with what looked like laser beams of light.

Then a Boeing 757 came by and met the same fate. I was lucky because I was flying low and relatively slow, trying to avoid being seen on radar by the authorities. I think that's why the alien craft didn't see me. That's how I ended up here. I did an emergency landing. I think it was my lucky day.

I'm sorry. But my plane will only carry three passengers. I'll get rid of the cocaine, and I'll take Scott, Karen, and Anne to Neiva. It's not far. I'll drop you off at the airport and come back for Alice and Louise. It's just not physically possible to carry all six of us because of weight restrictions, and I'm getting low on fuel.

'I will only be two hours or so,' Samuel says to Alice and Louise. 'I'll drop your three friends off and come back for you two. Stay in the shade. We'll leave you plenty of water. Don't worry. You'll be fine.'

Samuel tells them that this place, the Tatacoa Desert, was named by Spanish conquistadores in 1538, who named it the Valley of Sorrow. 'But for us, it is not a sorrowful place. It is a valley of hope and happiness,' he says, adding, 'We will all be fine, but we'd better make a start.'

Karen and Scott help Samuel unload the cocaine off the plane. Anne gives her two friends a big hug and kiss as she climbs on board, following the others. Samuel starts the plane's engine.

Anne starts to cry as the plane slowly moves away down the desert along the hard clay. Karen puts her arm around Anne and tries to comfort her. The plane starts to lift off and climb into the midday sky, and they've soon cleared the trees and are flying along at 1,000 feet.

Alice and Louise wave goodbye and watch the plane disappear into the distance. They hear the noise of the engine gradually fade away. Now only the noise of the breeze keeps them company.

On board the plane, Samuel was fascinated by his three passengers' stories of what they had been through. It seemed so unbelievable, but it was real.

Karen tells Samuel all about the base on the moon and the complex in the desert of New Mexico.

As Samuel listens to the horrific tales of the growing rooms, he's looking out the windows. He points out cars below that were attacked by the alien crafts. These burnt-out wrecks with charred bodies are scattered all around.

There are a few big trucks too, hardly recognisable. Samuel points out a school bus full of schoolchildren, all burnt to cinders. Only the frame of the bus remains, along with the bones and skulls of the children, scattered in the desert sands.

The farther they fly, the more smashed-up massive alien crafts they see, their wreckage strewn about the earth. A few—of those that had dropped off hordes of giant aliens— remain intact. And hundreds of giant dead aliens lie on the ground where they fell once they were affected by the virus Simon put into the clones they fed on. In the far distance, black smoke billows and fires burn.

'We'll be at Neiva in ten minutes,' Samuel announces.

Karen and Anne start to laugh and hug each other.

'Oh great,' Karen says. 'I can't wait to get back to a big city and get my feet back on the ground.'

As they approach the city, the destruction becomes more obvious; building after building was totally destroyed in the alien attack. Samuel lowers the plane, descending towards the airport. He can only just see through the smoke that all the runways were totally destroyed. Charred remains, barely recognisable as human, are scattered all around the city. Burnt-out vehicles and the rotting bodies of giant alien creatures, covered in swarms of flies, are strewn throughout the streets. Vultures are fighting over their stinking bodies. There is no sign of human life anywhere. This big city of Neiva, with a population of 370,000, has been completely destroyed.

Karen and Anne's joy soon turns to fear. Both are now hysterical crying, begging not to go down there.

'It's awful,' Karen cries, terrible. Please, Scott, don't make us go down there.'

'We have to,' Samuel says gravely. 'We have no choice. We're running very low on fuel.'

Scott tries to comfort the girls as best he can.

'We can't land at the airport,' Samuel tells them all. 'It's been destroyed. There are no runways left, and all of the city is gone too. I will have to find a place to land upwind, to avoid the smoke on the outskirts of the city.'

Samuel circles the ruins until he sees an empty strip of land just on the outskirts of the city. He brings the plane down to a perfect landing. They all clap and cheer with relief and excitement as they land in the field.

'I was hoping to land at the airport,' Samuel says. 'We need some fuel'.

'Come on,' Scott says. 'We'll have a look around and see if we can sort something out. We desperately need fuel to go back and get Louise and Alice.'

CHAPTER 14

THE VALLEY OF SORROW

Karen and Anne refuse to get out of the plane. They're both terrified of the giant dead aliens, the swarms of flies, and the vultures. The smell of burnt and rotting flesh is worse than anything they've seen or come across before.

Scott tells them both, 'Stay in the back of the plane, crouch down on the back seats, and don't move. Don't get out for anything until we get back!'

'Please be quick,' Karen replies. 'And don't worry. We won't leave the plane for anything.'

Scott and Samuel set off on foot, cautiously walking past the ruins and rubble, past all the charred human bodies and the rotting giant aliens.

Samuel is shocked at the size of the aliens. 'They must have been terrifying in battle,' he says to Scott.

'Yes,' Scott agrees. 'They're terribly frightening creatures. I've seen them eating body parts, arms and legs of the human clones on board the alien crafts when we travelled to earth from the moon. I also saw them running into battle, charging off the alien crafts on the first day of the invasion of the world.

Samuel approached the body of a dead alien. He could hardly breathe with the smell of the decaying body. He bent over it and removed its laser weapon. He aimed the laser at a phone booth across the road and fired a shot; the phone booth was instantly melted in a blinding flash.

'Wow! What a weapon,' shouts Samuel. 'You grab one too.'

Scott picks up one of the lasers.

'We don't know how bad things might get now law and order has broken down,' Samuel points out. 'People can be as bad as the aliens sometimes, especially when they have no law and order and no food or water.'

As they walk along the streets climbing over rubble and avoiding crumbling and burning buildings, Scott sees a Toyota Hilux pickup truck that looks to be in good condition in an underground car park. He points it out to Samuel.

When they walk over to it, they see that the door is slightly ajar, and the keys are still in the ignition. They look, but there seems to be no one about.

'Jump in,' says Scott.

They climb in, and Scott drives out of the car park.

'We need some fuel,' Samuel says. 'We have to get to the airport.'

They eventually make their way through all the mayhem and arrive at the airport. They find the fuel pumps and ascertain, to their relief, that the fuel stored underground is safe and ready to use. Samuel finds a big empty fuel drum, and they started to fill it up.

'We need forty-one gallons,' Samuel says. 'That's the

maximum the tanks will hold; it'll give us a range of 800 miles.

'That's good,' says Scott. 'What's the plane's speed?'

'It'll do 150 miles per hour,' Samuel tells him.

Once they get the drum filled, they put a hand pump and a shovel in the back of the pickup.

'Come on. We have got to hurry,' says Scott. 'I don't want to leave the girls too long.'

They jump back into the pickup and head back towards the plane on the outskirts of the city.

Scott remembers the way back around all the obstacles and is making good time. They're only about three-quarters of a mile from the plane when, suddenly, without warning, an army jeep comes flying out of a side street. The four men sat inside open fire on Scott and Samuel, peppering the pickup with a hail of bullets.

Samuel, acting instinctively, grabs his laser weapon, and in a flash, the jeep and its occupants are incinerated. In the chaos, Samuel doesn't realise he was shot and is now bleeding from his chest. Once the immediate threat has been eliminated, he feels something is off and looks down to see that he's losing blood rapidly.

'Hold on,' Scott calls, pressing his foot to the metal and driving as fast as he can to get back to the girls.

Karen and Anne had heard the shooting and the laser fire, and both are terrified, huddling together in the back of the plane.

Scott pulls up alongside the plane in a cloud of dust and slams on the brakes. He jumps out of the pickup, shouting, 'Karen! Karen!'

Karen and Anne climb out of the plane.

'Oh, I'm so glad to see you,' says Karen.

'What's wrong?' Anne asks. 'You look worried.'

'Samuel has been shot by a gang of men back in the city,' Scott tells them. 'We were ambushed by the first people we came across.'

Samuel is moaning in the front of the pickup truck. Karen looks in through the passenger window at Samuel, who is covered in blood. 'Oh, my God!' she cries.

'There is a first aid box in the front of the plane,' Samuel tells her.

She runs over to the plane and gets the first aid box.

Anne and Karen try their best to comfort Samuel and to stop his bleeding, but the wound is bleeding heavily, and it won't stop. Samuel is in a lot of pain, now that the shock is wearing off.

Karen leaves Anne to look after Samuel and whispers to Scott, 'I don't think Samuel is going to make it. It's not looking too good for him.'

Scott says, 'Oh, my God. No! Poor Samuel. He is a good man. I haven't known him long, but I've really gotten to like him. And we really need him to fly the plane. There is no way we can fly back for Louise and Alice without him.'

Karen goes back over to Anne to see if there's anything she can do to help. 'How is he?' she asks.

Anne is sobbing quietly, tears running down her face. 'I think he's dead,' she says quietly. She's holding Samuel's hand.

Karen starts to cry too. Scott checks Samuel's pulse, but there is no sign of life. He can't believe it. He was speaking to Samuel just ten minutes ago. He thinks about how fragile life is.

The three of them dig a grave for Samuel and burry him. Scott makes a cross and places it on the grave. Karen says a prayer, and they all stand in silence for a minute. It's the best they can do for Samuel.

'Well,' Scott says. 'We have to get back to the Tatacoa Desert to help Alice and Louise. We can't fly the plane, so we'll have to drive back. We can't leave them. They only have enough water for one day, especially in this baking heat.'

The three of them climb into the pickup truck and cautiously drive through the town. They collect food and water, finding what they can among the debris and ruins of the shops in the city.

Scott shows Karen and Anne how to use the laser weapon just in case they need to defend themselves. At first, they are a bit scared of the laser, but they both get used to it quickly. Scott is pleased with their progress. They soon got the hang of it, and Scott is pleased with their shooting ability. 'You're like modern-day Annie Oakley's,' he tells the girls.

They all have a little laugh, and they feel a little safer and a bit more confident.

They all get back into the pickup truck and head out of town, driving towards the Tatacoa Desert to get their friends. They figure it will take about two hours to drive back to Louise and Alice.

Scott does the driving. He hopes Anne's friends will be all right. They are going to be longer than they had intended, but it couldn't be helped.

It's a lovely day, with a nice breeze blowing, and the scenery is beautiful. They talk about life, their newfound freedom, and their futures. Anne talks about her family in Kent, telling Scott and Karen about the little village by the sea, where she lived with her parents and her younger brother. They ran the village shop and post office. She and her younger brother had a paper route together. Oh how she misses them all and wonders how they all are.

Karen talks about her parents in Las Vegas. She tells Scott and Anne about Tom, her father, a lovely man and a top lawyer at the firm where he works. She talks about her mother Paula, who is loving and caring and tells them of her lovely childhood. She grew up privileged and knows how lucky she was, living in a grand mansion with her dog, Bolo. A Cane Corso, he looked fierce, but he was loving. She would give the world to see them all again. She hopes to make them all proud by following in her father's footsteps and becoming a top lawyer at a big firm too.

Scott tells Karen and Anne about his life in his small town when he was young and his happy childhood. He talks about his job in the garage and the awful day when his parents died in a car crash and about Joe, his boss and friend. He hopes Joe and the town are all right.

The miles and the minutes fly by, and before they know it, Scott is announcing, 'We're getting close to the girls. I remember flying over here with Samuel in his plane. I remember that burnt-out school bus with all those bodies.

'Don't look,' Scott warns the two girls as they pass the wreckage once more. 'We're not far from Alice and Louise now. Keep your eyes open for them. They could be anywhere around here.'

Scott has slowed down to twenty miles per hour, and all three of them are looking out of the windows scouring the desert around them for any sign of their friends. All of a sudden, Anne shouts, 'Look over there!'

They can see two young women about one hundred yards away—lying motionless on the desert floor. Scott stops the pickup, and all three of them jump out and race over to the young women.

Their worst fears are met. They discover that it is Louise and Alice, but both are dead. It looks like they were attacked by a jaguar and partly eaten. Both of their throats were ripped out.

Karen and Anne are hysterical, screaming and in shock.

Scott drove them away so they can't keep staring at the grisly sight. He picks up his laser and walks back to the bodies. A few vultures have gathered around and are starting to eat the bodies. Scott fires his laser near the birds, and they screech and fly off into the desert sky.

He retrieves the shovel from the truck and digs two shallow graves, crying as he does so. When he's done with the digging, Scott buries Louise and Alice, putting a stone on the top of each grave. He walks back to the truck, thinking that, in the last couple of hours, they had lost three of their friends. They are living in dangerous times. He recalls what Samuel said—about the valley being a place of hope and happiness. Perhaps those who'd named it originally were right; it was, indeed, the Valley of Sorrow today.

Scott got back in the pickup truck and tells Karen and Anne that he had buried the two girls. They are heartbroken, and Scott tries to comfort them.

'We have no choice now,' he says. 'We'll have to drive to Las Vegas. We'll have to take it in turns driving. We could do four hours at a time each if that works for you both.

What do you say? I think it'll take about two and a half days in total.'

Karen and Anne agreed, and the three of them set off on their journey.

CHAPTER 15

THE EUREKA MOMENT

Back in the New Mexico desert above the complex where the human clones were grown, Simon and some of his colleagues have come across an alien craft. His colleagues worked in the fields of computers, linguistics, physics, and propulsion systems.

Andrew was one of the scientists who worked on a top-secret project for the US government. He'd been trying to crack the language of the aliens, but when the aliens thought he was getting close to cracking the meaning of their hieroglyphics and learning their language, they abducted him one night and took him to the complex.

The group of scientists, along with Simon, have been working on the alien craft for a couple of days. The craft is fully intact. It landed on the day of the invasion to drop the alien invaders off and has sat empty ever since, as its pilot and crew died from the virus shortly after disembarking.

The other scientists managed to turn on the power supply. When they did so, the whole of the inside of the craft lit up with a glowing yellow light, and the control panels all flashed into life. All the symbols on the screens look very similar to Egyptian hieroglyphs, and the group of scientists stared at the screens, unable to decipher what they were look at.

Since then, they'd all spent hours checking through loads of files. But the files remained meaningless to them— just a jumble of symbols and hieroglyphs. That is, they were until Andrew came across a file that contained a conversation between the US government and the aliens. The conversation was written down in English, but below it were the corresponding alien symbols and hieroglyphs; the conversation had been translated into the alien language.

Now the scientists can cross-reference the letters to the symbols and match the two languages up; they have found the way to translate the alien language. It's like finding the Rosetta stone.

Andrew now knows how to interpret the language, and he soon starts to learn all the controls. Before long, he has learnt all of the craft's systems and controls. Andrews starts to look through hundreds of files. With the discovery of the conversation, he realizes, he can now learn more in a few weeks than the human race could have learned in a thousand years without that key.

After a couple of days of working on the craft, John, one of the scientists who was part of Simon's group and worked on propulsion systems and physics, say to the other scientists, 'It's relatively simple to operate the craft. You just have to give the command to the master computer. Then it will send the message to the computer that deals with that request.

'Watch,' John says. 'I'll type in, "Close the doors."' He did so, and the doors all around closed.

He typed in, 'Start engine.' The engine started with a low-pitched humming noise so soft it was barely audible.

The team of scientists are amazed and excited. They all slowly start to get to know the controls. They realise the craft is operated by a highly advanced autopilot. All you have to do is type in the grid coordinate to wherever you want to travel, and the craft will transport you there. The whole of the known universe was mapped out; each galaxy has its own grid reference along with each solar system and then each planet.

Simon types earth into the computer, and a large hologram about ten feet in diameter appears in the centre of the control room. A layer of grid references is projected all over the massive hologram of the globe. 'This is unbelievable,' Simon says. 'The technology is so much more advanced than ours.'

'Look,' says John, 'it has different speed settings. There's intergalactic, interstellar, interplanetary and planetary.'

'Well,' Simon says, 'we will have to earn our wings.' He types in '62^D-79*' and planetary speed 1, the slowest speed. The coordinates represent Salt Lake City. 'Here we go.' He types in the command, 'Take off.' Up they fly, reaching 10,000 feet quickly and then zooming at supersonic speed across the desert. They got to their destination in half an hour. It's brilliant.

After they've spent some time hovering over Salt Lake City, John says, 'Let's get back to the complex.'

Simon types in the coordinates '61^D-72*'; sets the craft to planetary speed 10; and types, 'Go.' The craft shoots off at a tremendous speed, and they're back at the complex within ten minutes.

Simon and John disembark once they're back in the desert, while Andrew remains on board at the computers. He's combing through the files, looking at all the messages before the invasion to see if he can learn anything about the aliens.

After a while, Andrew comes running out of the craft, shouting, 'Simon! John! Come here quick.'

They both run up to Andrew. 'What's wrong?' asks John.

'I've just received a message from an alien craft,' Andrew tells them. 'It's in the Orion constellation, and it's asking how the invasion is going. They want to know when the earth has been conquered. Then they can start to colonise the earth.'

All three men run back on board. Andrew shows Simon and John 'I'm going to send a reply saying all is going well and the victory is nearly complete,' he tells them. 'I'll add that I'll send an update next week to let them know how things are going.'

He sends the reply and then says, 'I've narrowed down where the message came from.' He explains that the origins of the message are somewhere near Sigma Orionis, a star in the Orion constellation. 'There must be a planet near that star,' he says. 'I've typed in the coordinates for Sigma Orionis, and it's 1,072 light years away. But when I looked at the time it would take to travel there, it said two weeks— traveling at intergalactic speed 10. That is unbelievable! We would say impossible, but not with their technology.'

After a discussion, the three scientists start to form a plan. They have to warn the world—or what is left of it at any rate—of the impending danger. They set off in the craft, with plans to fly around the world. They head to Europe. When they got to Rome, hovering over the city, Simon looks through the windows. He can't believe what he finds. It looks like a nuclear explosion has destroyed it. Not a building is left standing. Symbols came up on the console to say it's safe to land—that no radiation or pollution has been detected.

Simon orders the craft to land. After it has made a safe landing, the doors open, and the three scientists exit the craft. It's eerily silent, and it looks like Hiroshima after the nuclear bomb was dropped on it. Nothing seems to be left; they can see no living humans and no animals; no birds are singing, and there are only dead people and aliens as far as they eye can see.

On their travels around the world, the three come across other alien crafts that are still intact. Andrew and John pilot two of them, and they fly in a convoy, along with Simon. Everywhere they go, they are a sight to behold. They scour Europe searching for survivors.

They came across crews of naval submarines from the world's navies and people from every walk of life. All told, the three crafts are filled with about 2,000 survivors by the time they headed back to the complex in the desert.

The three crafts land perfectly, and everyone disembarks from the alien crafts, full of joy and excitement at having survived the tragedy and trying to understand what they've all been through. Simon gathers everyone and he explains everything he knows about the aliens. He tells the people about the aliens' plans to come back and rule the world and asks for volunteers to fly the alien crafts. Among the survivors are fighter pilots, airline pilots, and military personnel, among them a general in the army and several officers from all across Europe. Altogether, there are about 200 volunteers.

Simon, Andrew, and John train the new pilots over the next few days. They show the trainee pilots how to operate the computers, how to set the destination, and how to use the weapon systems. The training is going well, and the new pilots are soon flying like they've flown for years. Simon sends them on missions, targeting old building and vehicles, and they practise firing the laser weapons and destroying their targets.

While the pilots are training, the rest of the people take on the job of cleaning out the complex. They get it all cleaned out and stock up on supplies; it is their underground fortress now.

The three scientists get their crafts ready for the next stage of the mission. The 200 new pilots are divided equally among them and put on board the three crafts. All head out in search of more abandoned alien crafts to bring back and boost their new air force. They came across more and more crafts, along with thousands more people from all over the world. And some of the crafts bring back food and supplies.

Soon, the crafts are taking off and landing day and night. The survivors have amassed a large force of crafts with hundreds of fully trained pilots and a fully stocked base—the fortress underground.

Some of the crafts were filled with laser weapons. When these land and the doors open, the weapons are handed out to everyone over sixteen, and all are trained up on how to use them. People from all parts of the world become part of the new world army.

CHAPTER 16

A MESSAGE TO THE STARS

As it grows dark and it starts to get cold, Simon gathers everyone together; there are loads of people—tens of thousands. 'I am going to have to inform the aliens that the world has been conquered,' he announces over a megaphone. 'That means telling them that it's all right to start the colonisation of the earth. I'm sorry,' he adds. 'But if I don't reply or if I tell them things aren't going well, they'll be suspicious and expecting trouble and will send a larger invasion force.'

He explains to the massive crowd that, once the alien force arrives, they'll all have to fight for the planet. 'For our world!' he cries. 'Because if we lose, it will be the end of humankind.'

The crowd shouts and cheers, the response growing louder and louder, building like a wave and spreading all around the huge crowd. 'Kill the aliens!' they chant. 'Kill the aliens!'

When the crowd eventually disperses, the people make their way down into the complex for the night. Andrew goes into his craft and sends the message to the aliens at Sigma

Orionis. 'The planet has been conquered,' it says. 'All the humans are dead. We have started to grow human clones on the surface. There will be no resistance. Welcome to our new world.'

A reply comes back quickly. 'Another great victory for our empire. Another home for us in the quest to conquer the galaxy. Well done! We will be setting off imminently.'

Andrew exits the craft and tells Simon what he's done. 'I couldn't wait any longer. They would have known something was wrong.'

Simon called a meeting with Andrew, John, and all the military leaders in his old office down in the complex. He tells them all about the experiments with the clones and the growing rooms and the human-animal hybrids. He adds that it was all done with the knowledge of the world's governments. They all swear an oath that nothing like that will ever happen again if they are successful in the war—that they will establish a safe new world for everyone.

They discuss the upcoming battle late into the night. Time is critical. The alien fleet is now on its way. Together, they work out a battle plan. One of the top men from the new air force, Lieutenant Colonel Stevens, says, 'We don't have a big enough force even with the element of surprise. We won't stand a chance. But we can't tell the people. There will be mass hysteria. We don't have time to repair the damaged alien craft even if we knew how. We have to keep searching the world for more survivors and intact alien crafts and keep training as many pilots as we can. We want only the best. Bring back weapons, food, and supplies. We have to be ready.'

A top military man from Britain, General Williams,

says, 'I want everyone to be trained on how to use the alien weapons.' He also wants the people put into fighting units. He tells the officers there to make the complex secure. 'I want trenches dug and fortifications all around the complex.' He gave the order to start first thing in the morning.

Lieutenant Colonel Stevens reiterates his concern. 'The initial conflict will go well for us because the aliens won't be expecting trouble. We'll have the element of surprise. But once they realise what's happening, it won't go too well for us.'

An RAF pilot among the group says, 'Remember the Battle of Britain. Never was so much owed by so many to so few,'

'Yes,' John says, 'that's the spirit. We can do it, or we will die trying.'

Eventually, the plans have been made and the meeting ends with John saying, 'We must all get some sleep, or we'll be no use for anything.'

They make their way back to their rooms along the massive underground complex, all of them thinking of the upcoming battle.

Morning comes, and the complex is a hive of activity. Groups of people are in training, with the army doing weapon training and tactical manoeuvres. Some of the young men are digging trenches and making defensive mounds all around their desert fortress. Hundreds of crafts are lined up all around the complex.

Simon goes out to his craft with his crew. He tells the other pilots and their crews to keep going out on missions to find as many people and usable crafts as they can. He reminds them that time is running out and tells them to destroy any alien crafts that can't be flown. That way, the alien invasion force won't see them.

Simon's craft, with its small crew, takes off from the desert. They fly slow, everyone looking out for people or usable alien crafts.

Suddenly, one of the laser gunners shouts out, 'Vehicle below.' Simon brings the craft down near the vehicle, and he and some of the crew walk over to the vehicle. Simon can see that there are three people inside and that they're terrified. Huddled in the foot well, the occupants are terrified, screaming, too frightened to even look out.

Simon opens the door of the vehicle. 'It's okay,' he says. 'Don't be afraid. We're human. We won't hurt you.'

CHAPTER 17

FRIENDS REUNITED

The people in the truck sit up. 'It's Simon,' says a voice.

It's Karen, and she's ecstatic, overjoyed to see a familiar face instead of an alien invader. She jumps out of the truck and puts her arms around Simon, giving him a big kiss and a hug. Scott and Anne jump out of the pickup truck and join in the group hug, laughing and crying tears of joy.

They all exchange their stories. Scott tells Simon how he and Karen escaped from the growing rooms, swapping places with the two clones and leaving on board the alien craft even though they didn't know where they were going—and how they could never have imagined they'd find themselves on a underground base on the dark side of the moon ruled by aliens.

Simon tells them how he poisoned the clones but wasn't sure if his plan had worked and how, when he saw some of the grey aliens in the complex dying, he'd ventured out. He was amazed to learn about the moon base and that there are thousands of human workers up there stranded.

'A lot of them are my friends,' Anne says. 'Please will you help them? Otherwise, they will all die up there.'

Simon assures her he'll do all he can to get the poor people off of the moon before it's too late for them. 'Come on,' he tells them. 'Get on board my craft.'

Once they're all on board, Simon heads straight back to the desert complex—their new fortress and the headquarters for their new world. On the way back, Karen introduces Anne to Simon.

They arrive back at the fortress, and Simon brings the craft down, landing in the desert. All around, crafts are taking off and landing—with new people arriving, along with more weapons, food, and supplies.

Simon leads everyone off the craft and down into his office down on Level 10. Karen remembers the last time she was there—back when she called Simon evil. She knows now that couldn't be further from the truth.

A big meeting is held with all the scientists and all the top military leaders. After a lot of discussion and debating, they decide to launch a rescue mission. Scott says, 'There might be many more alien crafts up there that we can use in the battle.'

The orders are given to assemble fifty crafts all crewed up, carrying ten trained pilots each. Simon, Scott, Karen, and Anne went in the lead craft. They all go into the control room. When Simon gives the order to take off, the others are astonished; they weren't in the control room when it was up and running. They had previously only been in the cargo hold. Simon types in the coordinates for the moon from the hologram of the solar system, they stand there in amazement. All the screens light up, Simon types in 'Take-off', and they fly off straight up into space. They travel at interplanetary 10 speed.

They're excited and ready to go back and rescue all the workers on the moon. This time, they're going to the moon for a good reason—and not to be slaughtered and eaten by aliens.

The massive crowd that gathered on the desert floor all shouted and cheered as they waved the rescue crafts goodbye; the crowd was celebrating in high spirits. They all looked on as the formation of crafts flew up and out of sight.

Now, Simon looks out of one of the windows, and he can see the Orion constellation. 'We don't have long now before the aliens come back with a massive force to colonise the earth and eradicate us from the face of the earth,' he says. 'If that happens, they will rear humans on farms—the first generation of humans born from clones. Then they will be reared free range on big open planes and then rounded up for slaughter when fully grown, now the world is clean.'

The fleet of fifty crafts are swiftly approaching the moon and then, just as soon, starting to go around the dark side of the moon.

'I can't wait to see all my friends again down there,' Anne says.

'I'm sure they will all be fine,' Karen tells her. 'We will soon have them all back on earth safe and sound.'

Anne smiles as Karen gives her a reassuring hug.

Lights start to flash on the control panels of the craft.

Simon says, 'The craft is going into landing mode. The computers are sending signals to the moon base to open up the craters so the crafts can go down into the city below.

The crafts start to descend into the massive city, which is all lit up. But there is no activity—not a thing moving around—and no noise whatsoever. All the workers went into hiding when they saw the crafts coming down to land; they thought the aliens had come back.

The crafts land in the city, and the crews, along with the 500 pilots, disembark and venture into the vast ultramodern city of glass and chrome. 'Hello!' they all started shouting. 'Hello! Anyone there? We are from earth. Come out. We mean you no harm!'

Scott, Karen, and Anne stay together. Eventually and slowly, the workers from the factory came out of hiding. Once they see the crafts have brought humans who've come to rescue them, they are elated. The workers kept coming out of their hiding places, looking dirty, thin and bedraggled; it's like liberation day in a war. They all go around the city gathering up more and more workers.

Simon, Andrew, Scott, and the 500 pilots leave the search for people and explore the city looking everywhere for alien crafts.

Simon tells everyone to meet up in the enormous city square. 'We will wait twenty-four hours, and then we must head back to earth and prepare for the battle before the aliens arrive.'

Over the next twenty-four hours, thousands of bedraggled and weary-looking workers gather. But now they have hope; they are going back to earth! Hundreds and hundreds of crafts are filling the city square. They eventually run out of pilots to man them. There is a great feeling in the air.

Simon climbs on top of one of the crafts. Standing on top of the roof, he rallies everyone around him, speaking to everyone there. 'We must go back to earth, our world,' he tells them, 'the home of us all. Whether black, brown, yellow, or white—whatever our colour, creed, or gender—we must fight the evil enemy that wants to take over our world and eat all our descendants. They will treat us worse than cattle. We will not go gently into that good night. We will rage—rage against the dying of the light.'

The crowd cheers, shouts, and claps.

'Come on,' Simon shouts. 'We're going back to earth, back to our home, to join the force down there.'

Everyone boards the crafts with great excitement. The pilots type in the coordinates 'Earth 61^D-72*'. The crafts lift up in a gigantic wave—the massive fleet of crafts all heading back to earth a heart-warming sight.

Andrew sends a message to the aliens who are on their way from sigma Orionis. They are racing through space and only a few days away from earth now. The message reads, 'The base on the moon of earth has been closed down. All the supplies and clones have been transferred to the earth. We will meet up at earth co-ordinates 61^D-72*.'

A reply came back. 'See you in three days' time in our new world. Long may our empire rule the galaxy.'

The earth comes into view. Upon seeing their home planet, all the people on the craft let out a collective gasp. They can't believe they're going back home. Joy fills the air.

Karen gives Scott a big hug and kisses him. 'We are going home. And this time, we're staying home,' she says, adding, 'and, I hope, staying together.'

Scott gives her a big kiss. 'Karen, we will always be together,' he tells her. 'I love you, and nothing can keep us apart.'

Karen's face lights up; a big smile spreads across her face.

The fleet of crafts come into the earth's atmosphere. The

people on board see the outline of America, which gradually grows larger. They start to descend into the New Mexico desert and soon come to rest at the side of the complex, where some thousand or so crafts are lined up in rows. The pilots and crews lead the workers off the crafts, and the new arrivals are greeted by everyone from the complex and made to feel at home. They're fed and shown to their rooms. They can all have a shower in the rooms where the human clones were once washed. But now, instead of screams and screeches, the rooms are filled with laughter and joy.

Anne and Karen tell Scott they want to go home to see if their families and parents are alive. Simon overhears them talking. He calls a meeting with everyone.

At the gathering held in the desert, there are about 250,000 people. Simon speaks over a large speaker system so everyone can hear. 'This force gathered here is voluntary,' he says. 'No one is forcing you to stay or to fight. We only want people here whose hearts are in the war. If anyone is wishing to leave or go home, we'll do our best to get you home. But we need you to stay if you feel up to it. I will be in my craft here tonight. Anyone wishing to leave, please come and see me. But whatever you decide to do, I wish you all well. Good luck and God bless you all. At least we are all back on earth and free to choose.'

The crowds of people are eating, drinking, and partying through the night. They're all just happy to be alive and free, making the most of their time before the aliens come back.

Only a few hundred people decide to leave; Karen and Anne are among them.

'I can't let you go by yourself,' Scott says to Karen. 'I'll come with you.'

CHAPTER 18

IS THERE ANYONE HOME

The night passed by so quickly the bright disc of the sun peaked above the desert horizon. Simon organises the transport for the people going home. There are so few of them he orders each person or group of people to have their own craft take them.

Simon tells Scott, Karen, and Anne that he will personally take them. Those on the crafts say an emotional goodbye to the people they're leaving behind, and the crafts set off in their own time, leaving at intervals all homeward bound.

Scott and Karen are in Las Vegas in a flash. Simon lands the craft in an open park.

'Thank you so much, Simon.'

She breaks down crying as she hugs Anne and Simon. She is sad and sorry to leave them both, but she really wants to go home and see if her parents are both all right.

Scott shakes Simon's hand. He thanks him for everything he has done for him and Karen. 'I'm sorry I won't be in the battle with you,' he says. Then he turns to

Anne and gives her a big hug and a kiss and wishes her luck finding her family.

Simon lowers the craft's doors. Scott and Karen walk down the ramps into the park; it's a beautiful day, and the sun is shining. They turn and wave goodbye with tears in their eyes. In a flash the craft is gone, and they stand their feeling utterly alone in a vast city.

Simon and Anne head to England, where Anne will be dropped off near her home soon. In other crafts around the world, other pilots have dropped their passengers off too and are heading back to the desert fortress and the new world army.

Simon sends a message to all the other crafts around the world, instructing them to destroy and vaporise any craft they come across that is damaged, so the incoming alien invasion doesn't see them and become suspicious. He tells everyone to stay out of sight after tomorrow night, as all humans are supposed to have been exterminated.

All the crafts make their way back to the desert fortress, once they've taken their passengers to their respective homes. The pilots execute last-minute flying manoeuvres and participate in mock dogfights, the gunners on board practising their shooting. The army regiments are all ready now; all the medics and civilians know their jobs.

***

Back in Las Vegas, Scott and Karen make their way through the park and into the streets. 'It seems so strange,' Karen says. 'The last time I was in this park, it was filled with families and children playing.'

They leave the park and make their way through the

empty streets. Soon after they come across a car that has been abandoned, Karen drives through the ruined desolate streets. 'I thought I would someday take you to meet my parents on our date,' Karen says. 'I really liked you. But I never thought it would be under these circumstances. It's not looking too good. We haven't seen a sign of life yet.'

'I hope we find them safe and well, Karen,' Scott replies. 'But please prepare yourself for the worst. The chances of finding them alive and well are slim. I don't want to build your hopes up. Please prepare yourself for the worst. I'm so sorry, love.'

They pull up to the massive wrought iron gates of a mansion. 'We're here,' Karen says. 'This is where I live!'

'Wow! Very nice. It's beautiful,' says Scott.

Karen punches the code into the keypad for the automatic gates, and they slowly start to open. Karen's heart is beating wildly; there've been times in the recent past when she never thought she would see this day. She starts to drive up the long winding drive.

She brings the car to a stop at the front of the house, and they both get out of the car and walk up the stone steps to the big oak doors. Karen opens the big heavy doors and walks in. 'Come on, Scott. Come on in,' she says.

Scott follows her in, looking all around. They're in a big open foyer, with a large crystal chandelier hanging from the high ceiling and nice oil paintings decorating the walls. A large open staircase stands about twenty feet directly in front of them. The only sound is the tick, tock ... tick, tock of a grandfather clock in the far corner.

'Hello, Mum!' shouts Karen. 'Hello Dad!'

No reply comes.

Karen and Scott make their way through the large house, calling out and searching in every room. Karen becomes more and more despondent with every empty room they come across. By the time they've finished they've found more empty rooms than Scott can remember, Karen is shaking and crying. Scott puts his arm around her, and they walk into the garden.

'We have to keep looking,' Karen says through her tears.

Scott shouts, 'Hello! Hello!'

He hears a rustling in the bushes and see the bushes part. Out bounds a giant black dog, barking and growling.

'Bolo, no!' shouts Karen. 'Bolo, sit.'

Karen's beloved dog looked well—so well, in fact, that it's clear he's being looked after and fed. A Cane Corso, which is a type of mastiff, Bolo is a big powerful dog, but he's gentle as a lamb if he knows you. And once he knows you, he is a friend for life. Karen makes a big fuss over Bolo, stroking and patting him as Bolo licks her and playfully pats her with his big paws.

While Scott and Karen are playing with Bolo, they hear a shout. 'Hello! Hello! Who's there?' It's Karen's dad. He comes barrelling out from behind a rhododendron bush brandishing a shotgun.

The gun drops as soon as he sees her. 'Karen! Karen!' he cries. 'You're alive!' He runs up to her and throws his arms around her. 'I thought I would never see you again.'

Karen's mum hears the commotion and comes up the garden from the summer house, where they've been living since the attack, as it is much more secluded than the big house—barely visible among the big trees and shrubs.

Karen's mum is in floods of tears as soon as she sees

Karen. 'Oh, my Lord. Thank God you're alive,' she says, holding Karen tightly.

They all stand together, crying and hugging each other.

After a minute or two, Karen turns to Scott. 'This is my mum and dad, Paula and Tom,' she says.

'Who is this young man?' Tom asks.

Karen answers, 'It's Scott, my boyfriend.'

'Pleased to meet you, Scott,' Tom says. 'Where on earth have you been? We've been worried to death about you.'

Karen replies, 'Dad you're going to find everything I'm about to tell you hard to believe.'

'Well try me love,' he says. 'I've heard some tales in my time in the courtroom. And after what I've witnessed these last few weeks, I can believe anything. Nothing will surprise me.'

Karen went on to tell her mum and dad everything that had happened since her first date with Scott. Taking it all in, they stand there in disbelief and horror.

'So are all the aliens dead now?' Tom manages to ask.

'Yes,' Scott tells him, 'all the aliens on earth and on the moon are dead. But there is a force on its way now; they'll arrive in just two days. We've managed to assemble a massive fleet of about a thousand of their crafts, all fully maned and with crews trained to defend us. The crafts are amazing, and their weapons are unbelievable.'

Paula gives Karen another hug and kisses her. 'I don't know how you managed to survive all that you've been through, down in the growing rooms and on the production line on the moon,' she says.

Scott tells Tom, 'This will be the last night of freedom. After tonight we must stay in hiding. The invasion will begin.'

Tom takes Scott up to the house. The two of them sit down in big leather chairs in the study. Tom gets a large bottle of whisky and a couple of glasses. He pours them both a drink. 'Cheers,' says Tom.

'Cheers,' Scott says. 'Here's to celebrating our reunion.'

Karen and Paula have gone down to the summer house to chat and let the men talk. They walk back up to the house after about twenty minutes to find Tom and Scott getting on well and chatting away.

Paula says to Karen, 'Go on, love. Tell him.'

Karen says to Scott, 'I need to talk to you in private, love.'

The two of them go out into the garden; it's a lovely sunny afternoon. The trees are gently blowing in the light breeze, and there isn't a cloud in the sunny summer sky.

Scott says, 'What's wrong, love? Are you all right?'

'Well, Scott I'm urrr,' Karen answers, faltering. And then, gathering herself, she says, 'I'm pregnant. I didn't know how to tell you. And I didn't want to tell you earlier with everything that was happening, but I think it's best that you know now.'

Scott is overjoyed. 'I'm so happy I'm going to be a dad! Are you okay with it, Karen?' he asks.

'Yes I am, love. Among all this death and destruction, new life will carry on. I'm sure we will win the war with the alien forces. We'll have our baby, and it will be one of the first to be born in the free new world.'

'What will Tom and Paula think of you being pregnant?' Scott asks. 'And what will they think of me?'

'My mum is telling Dad now,' Karen replies. 'My mum

is over the moon. I'm not so sure about Dad. But we will soon find out.' She has a big smile on her face.

Tom is a tall man, about six foot four. He's well built, about 280 pounds, very well spoken, and mild-mannered. At 55 years old, he wears his greying hair short. Until the invasion, he had a very happy life with his wife, Paula. She is a slim five foot three, weighing 128 pounds and looks younger than her 50 years. Her hair is collar length and blond, and she is always very well dressed. They are a happy couple, and Karen is their only child.

Tom and Paula walk hand in hand down into the garden from the house towards Karen and Scott. Big smiles shine on their faces, and Tom says, 'We're so happy for you both. He adds that he knows Scott will look after Karen and the baby because of the way he has looked after her up until now. 'After the battle, if all goes well,' he adds, 'we'll have a big wedding, the biggest party ever with all your friends from back at the desert fortress.'

They all sit out in the garden well into the night talking about the baby and the things they had been through and making plans for the future. It is a lovely clear night, and the stars are out.

Scott looked up at Orion high up in the summer night sky. He started to wonder what's happening out there. How far away were the alien invaders? How many of them would be coming?

They all had a nice night reminiscing and laughing, eventually heading back to the big house, as it gets cold. They go up to bed, all sleeping happy.

***

Morning comes so fast, Scott can hardly believe it. Time is flying. Scott remembers what Simon said about not going out from now on, so he tells everyone he thinks it best they all stay in from now on.

They pass the day indoors playing cards and looking at old photographs. Paula plays the piano, and they all have a good sing-song, trying to keep their spirits up and their minds off the impending invasion.

It is totally silent outside, except for the sound of the birds singing. Paula and Karen go into the kitchen to make everyone a coffee. Just as they do so, everything goes totally silent outside; all the birds stop singing. Bolo lets out a low-pitched growl and seems very restless.

Though it's only 6 p.m., it starts to grow dark. Normally, it would stay light until about 10 p.m. this time of year.

CHAPTER 19

RETURN OF THE ALIENS

Karen and Paula come back into the lounge carrying trays with drinks and cake. 'What's happening?' asks Paula. 'Is there going to be a storm?'

Scott and Tom are looking through the big bay window. 'They're here!' Scott says. 'The aliens have arrived.'

Paula and Karen drop the trays with a crash and stand there in disbelief and fear.

The sky is black as far as they can see—absolutely full of alien crafts. Never did Scott imagine the aliens would send so many crafts. There are crafts of all sizes, some as big as ocean liners, and they came in all shapes and sizes.

Scott thinks to himself, *We don't stand a chance. It's over.* But he tries to stay strong and reassure Karen and her parents. He knows that Simon and the earth's forces gathered by the complex will be able to see the alien invasion approaching.

***

Back in the desert, the military, Simon, and the scientists are all on board. The crafts and their crews are ready. The gunners man the laser guns. All are waiting for the battle to start—waiting for the time to strike with all their pent-up rage and fury. It will be payback time for the evil race of aliens.

The earth gradually darkens as the alien crafts get closer. They fill the sky, blocking out the sun like a gigantic swarm of locusts. The aliens think it's only a matter of landing on the earth and taking it over without any resistance. They aren't prepared for what is about to meet them. It will be like flying into hell.

The first few alien crafts land out in the desert. As they do so, Lieutenant Colonel Stevens gives the order to all the earth's forces to attack. 'Attack!'

They all shoot up to engage the aliens. In a flash, the earth's forces are shooting down the aliens; before they know what's happening, hundreds of the alien crafts have been shot down, blown out of the sky. The element of surprise worked. A few of the alien crafts manage to land, and the giant aliens come bounding off the crafts. But they are all cut down by the new world army, who shoot the aliens with their laser weapons.

There are thousands of men and women all in their trenches and behind the barricades. This time, the world is ready, and it is the aliens caught by surprise and lured into an ambush. The alien giants keep storming out of the crafts, bounding towards the new world army. And they are burnt to ashes and incinerated, as all the people shout and cheer.

The aliens soon realise what's happening, and they regroup and start to fight back. Simon is at the controls of his craft. In the first five minutes, he and his crew have managed to shoot down several crafts, but they're coming under fire now, with a few near misses. All around, there are dogfights in the sky, with crafts from both sides being shot down and falling like rain.

More and more alien crafts are landing far out in the desert, where the alien giants can land unchallenged and attack the new world army from all sides. The army officers have trained the people well in a short time, but they're no match for the alien giants, who have fought battles all around the galaxy and are battle hardened. Eventually, the tide turns in favour of the aliens. The alien giants are in among the people, jumping into the trenches and jumping over the barricades, ripping the people apart with their bare hands. It turns into a massacre. The alien giants are like ants swarming everywhere. For every alien killed, two more take its place.

The battle in the sky isn't going well either. Most of the crafts manned by the earth's pilots are shot down too. Simon gives the order to retreat; after an hour of battling, only about fifty of the earth's force are left flying.

Simon gives the order. 'Follow me! To the moon! They all shoot up into space, heading back to the moon base.

The aliens think they have won. The alien crafts are still arriving. Only now they're landing all over the world, with massive cargo ships, supplies, and weapons.

From up on the moon, Simon and the last fifty pilots and crew members can see a long line of alien crafts stretching far out to space as far as the eye can see. Hundreds of crafts are heading to earth from Sigma Orionis.

Simon, the pilots, and the crews have a meeting, and Simon tries to rally them all. 'We will all probably die,' he says. 'But we will have one last attack. We can't leave the last few people on earth to die. We must try to do something to help them or die trying.' It was like the charge of the light brigade.

All the crafts led by Simon fly in formation back to the fortress in the desert. They launch their suicide mission, attacking everything in their way with no concern for their own safety—cargo crafts, alien fighting crafts, and supply crafts are all destroyed.

The battle doesn't last long. Within twenty minutes, the last hope of humanity is shot out of the sky. Simon and the pilots are all killed trying to save the world. They all die bravely.

All is quiet around the world. Small groups of people are being hunted down and killed; it will only be a matter of days, and there will be no humans left on earth.

***

Scott has seen the fighting in the sky over in the desert and over Las Vegas. He can see what has happened. The battle is lost, the war is over. The world has been overrun by the aliens. Scott takes Tom to one side and tells him the outcome of the battle.

'We need somewhere to hide,' he says. 'Is there anywhere we can go? We must find somewhere quickly.'

'When I was a young boy, my father had a nuclear shelter built,' Tom says. 'He was terrified of the threat of a nuclear war between the USA and the USSR. It's in the garden under the summer house. He had the summer house built on top of the entrance to the bunker. That's why I talked Paula into heading down there. But she's terrified of the shelter. She won't go down it. There's a trap door that leads down to the bunker. My father made me promise that I would keep the bunker in good order, so every year on the anniversary of his death, I check it over and restock anything that needs replenishing. I keep my promise to him. I always thought he was an intelligent man.'

Scott gathers Tom, Karen, and Paula. 'Come on,' he tells them. 'We have to go to the shelter! Come on, Paula! If you don't go down there, you will die; you will never see your grandchild.'

They all run out of the house, through the big oak doors, and into the garden towards the summer house. As Karen is running she glances up into the sky. In the distance, about a thousand feet high, a group of alien crafts are slowly but steadily heading towards them. 'Oh my God!' she screams, dropping to her knees in terror.

Scott stops. He picks her up and carries her, and they all tear through the garden, their sights set on the summer house.

They all arrive safely, and Tom opens the trap door. Scott helps Karen and Paula down the steps and then walks back up to help Tom close the big shelter doors.

As Scott is about to help Tom close the doors, he looks up and sees two alien crafts directly overhead, only fifty feet above them. All of a sudden, he feels a big bang against his leg; it's Bolo barging his way past and running down into the shelter.

Scott and Tom struggle to close the big, heavy steel doors, pulling with all their might. They see the whole of the sky light up in a bright blinding flash of light. Then a massive *bang* shakes the ground beneath their feet, as if they're in the path of an astronomical earthquake.

The pair look up to see a gigantic mushroom cloud rising up to space. They close the doors behind them and go down into the shelter.

All around the world, nuclear missiles are raining down, and mushroom clouds are rising up into the atmosphere. Firestorms rage out of control, incinerating everything in their path, with 500 miles per hour winds destroying anything the fires don't hit.

All the aliens are killed. All the humans on earth are killed. Scott and Tom explain to Paula and Karen what they've seen just before they slam the shelter doors shut. But who or what could have done it?

CHAPTER 20

THE SHELTERED LIFE

In the shelter, the four are in utter shock, hardly believing what they just witnessed. They sit in silence for what seemed like ages. Then Karen says with tears in her eyes, 'What now, Dad? What do we do now?'

'I never thought anything like this would happen,' Tom says. 'I thought it would have been a war between America and Russia—maybe a conventional war with just a few nuclear strikes from either side before they both come to their senses.'

Karen starts to cry. 'What about my baby?' she asks. 'How long will we have to stay down here?'

Tom replies, 'I have enough supplies in terms of water and food to last six months. I have enough fuel to run the generator for lights, heating, and cooking for six months too. I thought two months would be the maximum time we would have to spend down here in a conventional nuclear strike. But I'm not too sure, having just seen what has happened. It looked like they were trying to destroy the whole world.'

'So how long? How long do we have to stay down here, Dad!?' screams Karen.

Scott holds Karen in his arms. He tries to comfort her and reassure her. 'Please calm down, love. You're getting hysterical. Don't get upset. Relax. Think of our baby. You managed to survive down in the complex in the desert in the growing rooms with all the clones. This is much better. You'll be clean and well fed. You have your family around you. We will all be fine, love. We have come through much worse and survived.'

'Yes, Karen,' Paula says. 'Scott's right. Calm down. We'll be fine. Your baby comes first. Put your faith in your father. All will be well.'

Tom nods in agreement. 'Yes, yes we will be fine,' he says.

They are all emotionally and physically drained. Tom shows them all around the shelter. It's brilliant and would put most hotels to shame.

'Wow. It's amazing,' says Scott.

Paula says, 'We'd all better get some sleep now. We've had a long, hard day. Let's get some sleep. We'll feel better in the morning.'

They all settle down, knowing they're safe from the alien threat; it will just be a matter of waiting until the levels of radiation are at a safe level. They sleep well and feel much better after a good sleep and once they've accepted the situation.

Scott and Karen have a nice room with a big double bed; the room was made to look like a log cabin. There's a 'log-burning' fire that is ornamental but looks nice and gives off heat. It looks so real.

Tom has made a great job of the shelter. He had put in televisions that can play DVDs and music, and there is an Xbox, as well as a PlayStation. In addition, there's a well-stocked library of books and films—enough to occupy them for months.

There is hot and cold running water, and they even have an ultra-modern shower room with a bathroom and toilet.

'Karen, come on,' Tom shouts. 'Breakfast is ready.'

'We're coming, Dad,' Karen calls as they make their way down the corridor from their bedroom down to the kitchen. They walked down the narrow corridor. The walls are covered in family photos and paintings of the family going back generations.

When they get to the kitchen, they're greeted with a big smile and a hug from Paula and the aroma of a nice home-cooked breakfast.

'Good morning, Paula. Good morning, Tom,' says Scott. 'What an amazing place you have here.'

'Well thank you. Now tuck into your breakfast before it goes cold,' replies Tom.

They sit eating breakfast, laughing and joking and in a much better mood now.

'Come on,' Tom tells Scott. 'I'll show you the rest of the shelter.'

Tom notes as he's giving the tour, 'I have my father to thank for all of this. He had it built in the early 1960s. He was so sure that one day it would be needed. He made me promise to keep it in good condition and fully working. I've kept it stocked with food and supplies all these years, and I'm so glad that I did now. I'm so grateful that I listened to my dad. He was a wise man.

While the men looked around, Karen and Paula did the washing up in the kitchen. They chatted away, making plans for the baby's future. They went into the living room and put a film on the television. Bolo sat on the rug by their side.

Soon, Tom had shown Scott all around the shelter—except for a small room at the back of the shelter. It was a room that recorded the outside conditions above ground, twenty feet above them. It had instruments that measured wind speeds, temperature, and rainfall, as well as a Geiger counter to measure the radiation levels on the surface.

Tom took Scott in and showed him around. 'Look, Scott. The radiation levels are 6,000 millisieverts (MSV). If you were to go outside now, Scott, you would be dead within a month. It's at the level that the Chernobyl nuclear reactor was at just after the reactor exploded. We need to wait until it gets down below 1,000 MSV. When that happens will depend a lot on where the explosions occurred and whether they were air bursts or detonated on impact. The weather conditions and wind speed and direction will make a big difference to the levels of radiation. We'll check the levels every week. Who knows how long it will take to come down to a safe level? But I hope not long.'

The days and weeks went by. Scott and Tom kept checking the levels.

It was good news after nine weeks—the counter read 1,150 MSV. It was getting close to the safe limit—at which point they could leave the shelter and go outside again.

The men made their way back to Paula and Karen, who were watching a movie in the living room.

Later that evening, when they were all having their evening meal, Tom tells them all that, at the rate the radiation was falling, it will only be two weeks and it will be all right to go outside—and leave the shelter.

Paula and Karen are so happy they cry tears of joy. They all have a big party and celebrate long into the night, knowing that the food and drink rationing won't be a problem.

'I can't wait to go back home,' says Paula.

'Me too. We can get the baby's room ready!' says Karen.

Tom thinks to himself, *I hope so*. But he's not sure what they will come out of the shelter to find. He doesn't want to dash their hopes, so he doesn't say anything.

They all sleep well that night, knowing the end is in sight.

Time goes by, and before they know it, two more weeks have passed. They go down to the monitoring room with all the measuring instruments together. It's the first day that it's stopped raining since they've been down there. It's warm too—seventy degrees. And a gentle breeze is blowing. The radiation level is at 920 MSV.

'Safe to go out!' shouts Tom.

Karen cries out, 'Hurray! Come on. Let's get out of here. Let's go home!'

'Just wait a minute, Karen,' Tom says. 'We have to prepare ourselves. Things might not be the same out there; the world might not be the way we left it .'

CHAPTER 21

A NEW BEGINNING

They all walk from the monitoring room down the corridor and arrive at the bottom of the stairs that lead up and out to the outside world. They stand there expressionless, in silence, each wondering what it will be like to open those doors.

Tom finally says, 'Come on, Scott. Let's get the doors open.'

They climb the stairs and start to open the doors. It's morning, and the sun is shining. There isn't a cloud in the sky. Bolo shoots up the stairs and barges past them all, heading outside. Running around, the great dog is oblivious to all that has happened.

They hold hands as they walk out into the bright sunlight. It takes a minute for their eyes to get used to the light. Eventually, they look to the house. But it's gone. There's nothing—nothing at all—no ruins, no grass, no trees, just bare earth. There's no noise at all, no birds singing, no life at all. It's a barren landscape as far as they can see.

They fall to their knees in shock and disbelief.

Karen and Paula are heartbroken. Huddling together,

they cry uncontrollably. Tom and Scott try to console them, but it's no use. Nothing they say or do can reassure them.

After a while, they climb a nearby hill that looks over the surrounding area. When they get to the top of the hill, it's just the same as far as they can see—nothing, just bare ground for at least ten miles in all directions.

'This is unbelievable,' Tom says. 'I never thought it would be so bad. It's like the end of the word—as if humankind never existed. All life on earth seems to be gone. There are no animals or birds and no people. We could be the last life on earth.'

They all make their way slowly back to the shelter. Downcast, heartbroken, and dejected they walk in silence, looking like the walking dead. They don't know what to do. It won't be long before all the food, water, and fuel will be gone.

Tom is upset and depressed. He isn't thinking right. When he gets back to the shelter, he goes into his bedroom, opens a bottle of whisky, and starts drinking. He drinks most of the day. He isn't thinking straight and decides to put an end to it all. Going to a drawer in his desk, he retrieves a shotgun and makes his way to where the others are gathered. He points the loaded gun at Paula and says, 'Forgive me. I can't let you all suffer and die of starvation I'm doing this because I love you all.'

'No! No!' Paula screams. 'We will find a way out of this, love.'

Bang! Tom pulls the trigger, and Paula falls down dead. Karen screams, 'Dad, no! What are you doing?!'

Tom turns the gun on her and Scott. Tom is just about to pull the trigger when Bolo comes bounding in and knocks him over. He falls to the floor, but he manages to pick the gun up and turns it on himself. *Bang*! Tom has shot himself. He lies there in a pool of blood—dead.

Karen screams, 'Oh, my God. How can this all be happening?'

Scott comes and holds Karen. They both stand there holding each other in floods of tears.

In less than an hour, they've gone from the joy of getting out of the shelter to the horror of the shootings and the death of Tom and Paula.

Karen is a total wreck; she's heartbroken. Scott takes her to the bedroom and tells her to sleep and get some rest. She's exhausted, and it's not long before she's fast asleep.

Scott walks around the shelter looking at the photos in the hall. His mind won't rest; a thousand things are going through his head.

He is so exhausted, both mentally and physically, that he cuddles up to Karen and falls asleep. Bolo lies in the room with Tom and Paula, staying by their sides all night.

The next morning, Scott wakes up early. Karen is still asleep. Scott wonders if it's all been a bad dream—until he goes into the living room and sees Bolo lying by Tom and Paula's bodies.

Oh no. Lord give me strength to do this please.

He goes back out of the shelter, takes a shovel, and digs two graves. He puts covers in the bottom of them and lays Tom and Paula to rest.

Upset, he makes his way into the kitchen to make a drink. As he's sitting there drinking his coffee, he hears Karen calling him. 'Scott, Scott, where are you?'

'I'm here, love, in the kitchen. Don't worry,' says Scott.

'Oh, Scott. I can't believe all this has happened. Where is Mom and Dad?' asks Karen.

Scott isn't sure what to say but tells her what he's done. 'We'll give them the best funeral we can under the circumstance,' he says.

'Yes, Scott, you're right,' she says. She finds her dad's Bible and some artificial flower wreaths that look real. She sprays them with mum's favourite perfume.

They go to the graveside and look at Tom and Paula lying at rest. They look peaceful. Karen places the flowers in the graves. Scott says the Lord's Prayer and then reads Psalm 23.

'Rest in peace, Mum. Rest in peace, Dad,' Karen whispers.

Scott comforts her. Bolo sits with them; it's like he feels their pain and loss.

Karen drops to her knees and looks to the heavens. She starts to pray. As she does, she sees a bright glowing disc approaching silently at about a hundred feet above them. It stops directly above them.

'What's that?' Karen asks Scott. 'Are the aliens back again?'

Before Scott can answer, a bright beam of light comes out of the glowing disc. It lifts them up, on a beam of light and they gently float up to it and pass through its walls.

Scott and Karen stand inside the glowing disc. It's filled with beautiful lights like the Northern Lights, dancing and flickering, and the most beautiful music they've ever heard. Then they notice a group of tall beings dressed in long white robes coming towards them. The one at the front, who seems to be the leader says to Scott and Karen, 'My children, have no fear. We mean you no harm. We are your guardians. We have been the guardians of humankind since the beginning of time. We have intervened several times in history. When the dinosaurs became extinct due to a giant meteor impact, we took you away to another planet until it was safe to bring you back to your home, the earth. That was why there was no record of you humans inhabiting the earth for millions of years.

'When the great flood came, we helped Noah and his family. They were on this craft with us and the animals of the world. We had all their DNA stored on our craft and then repopulated the earth.

'This will be the last time. We couldn't sit by and watch those evil creatures rule your world and farm you for their food. So, this is the end of this world—the end that has been talked about for thousands of years. Judgement Day is upon humankind. This world has ended. We'll take you to a new world known to you as heaven. All will be well for you. Humankind's destiny has been fulfilled.

Shortly after, they arrive at a new beautiful world. Scott, Karen, and Bolo are beamed down to the new world. Scott's mum and dad are there. Karen's mum and dad are there too. And Scott recognised people from the photos that were down in the shelter, all of Karen's family. Everyone is in the best of health. They'll all spend the rest of eternity in the most beautiful place imaginable, heaven!

One of the tall beings in all white says in a loud voice, 'This is not the end but just the beginning of a wonderful adventure.'

Printed in the United States
by Baker & Taylor Publisher Services